The Druid Queen

K. S. Gerlt

The Druid Queen

Book Cover by Lesia

Paperback ISBN: 978-1-965196-04-5

Hardcover ISBN: 978-1-965196-05-2

For the family we choose, and who choose us.

Astrid

My medicine bag slammed against my hip as I rounded the corner, and I grimaced at the sound of the precious glass vials clinking together. I could not afford to lose a single remedy, but I could also not afford to get caught. My footsteps echoed loudly in the deserted streets, and windows shuttered at my approach. Well, more like at the approach of my pursuers.

I risked a glance behind me and cursed under my breath at what I saw. The three tribesmen were still right on my tail, and quickly gaining on me. But at least Tariq was not among them this time.

Almost every time I had ventured beyond the guildhouse to treat someone afflicted with the plague, patrolling tribesmen had caught sight of me and given chase. Thanks to their mirage magic, they looked like regular Astorians until I could get close enough to see the slight distortion in the air around them, like the heat above a roaring fire. Because of that, I and every other true Astorian now eyed each other with wary suspicion, fearful that a word of dissent would land them in the tyrant's dungeons.

I picked up the pace, almost running into a raven-haired girl and her large dog. I nearly faltered when I sensed a hint of strange magic from the pair, but was spurred on by the thundering footsteps behind me. I sprinted around the last corner and into a dark, but familiar alleyway. I raced for the very back of the supposed dead-end, and reached for the ladder that we kept hidden behind a stack of empty crates.

My fingers found only empty air.

I frantically looked all around the dark alley for the ladder as the men closed in on me and panic crawled up my throat. Where had the ladder gone? It had been here only two days ago, the last time I needed to make a quick escape. Had the tribesman taken the ladder to prevent me from escaping them the next time they spotted me? But I had been *sure* to hide it!

"Looking for your ladder? I fear you will not find it here," sneered the lead tribesman as he entered the alleyway, his large frame blocking my only path of escape. "There is nowhere left for you to run, little rabbit."

I glanced at the stack of crates, wondering if they would hold my weight. They only reached a third of the way to the roof: Even if I jumped, I doubted I would be able to pull myself up onto the rooftop.

I had forgotten my bow and quiver in my rush to reach the victim before the plague claimed her. If I got through this, I vowed to strap it to my back during every waking moment.

"Is that what you think?" I said slowly, stalling for time.

I slowly turned to face the tribesman, drawing my dagger from its sheath. My other hand crept into my satchel while his eyes were pinned to my blade instead. Perhaps I could throw one of my powders into his face and dart past him before he could clear his eyes.

As he lumbered towards me, I quietly popped the cork off the vial, while keeping his attention on my weapon. My heart hammered against my ribs.

"I think," he drawled, "that this little rabbit is a runner, not a fighter." He advanced, closing the distance between us.

Just as I was about to hurl a handful of powder into his face, shouts rang out from the two tribesmen who stood at the mouth of the alley, and a dark blur raced down the alley towards us. I backed up as the large dog I had seen earlier put itself between me and the tribesman. It bared its fangs at him and growled a clear threat.

The big man froze, eyeing the canine worriedly. Now that I got a closer look at the animal, it was far too large to be a dog. No, my protector was clearly a wolf. But what was a *wolf* doing in the middle of the city, so far from the Druidlands?

"Hurry! Climb up!" cried a voice from behind me. I turned in surprise to see the raven-haired girl from before kneeling on the edge of the roof above me.

She threw down a rope ladder, and I wasted no time. I sheathed my dagger and lunged for it, climbing up the coarse rope as quickly as I could. I heard a snarl, cursing, and then a whimper from behind me, but I did not stop to look until the girl had hauled me over the lip of the roof. I finally looked down as she reeled the rope back up, out of reach of the tribesman, who was now bleeding heavily from a bite wound in his meaty forearm.

He glared up at us, and after glancing at the precarious stack of crates and coming to the same conclusion I had about its sturdiness, spat on the ground and turned to leave. The wolf growled and snapped at his retreating back, but I could tell by the way it stood that it was favoring one of its forelegs.

"Thank you for your help." I turned to my savior and held out my hand, and after a moment of hesitation, she shook it. For a moment, her dark eyes brightened to a vivid red, startling me. The moment she released my hand, however, her eyes went back to their darker hue.

"My pleasure." She gave me a slight smile, and I fingered my starsteel ring thoughtfully. "I would be lying if I said that I was a fan of the desert-dwellers."

"You and the rest of the kingdom." I returned her smile. "Was that your wolf?"

"Yes," she said after a moment of hesitation. "Yes, he is. His name is Rafe, and mine is Adelaide."

"Astrid. Please allow me to treat Rafe—I think he might have hurt his paw protecting me." The wolf looked up at me, as if he knew we were talking about him. His golden eyes seemed unnervingly intelligent.

"I would appreciate that." Adelaide bobbed her head in thanks. "Do you have a safe place where we could go?"

I paused for a moment, wondering if it were wise to bring her back to the guild. She was certainly not a tribeswoman in disguise, but she clearly had her own secrets. I supposed the enemy of my enemy was my friend, as the old saying went.

"Yes—we can go over the rooftops to get there. But...will Rafe be able to follow us there?" I glanced down at the wolf once more.

"He can follow my scent, and the sound of my voice." She looked down at him, and he almost seemed to nod.

"Wonderful. Then follow me." I stood up carefully and held out my hand to help her up. As I picked my way across the wooden shingles, I asked casually, "Did you just recently arrive in Astoria?"

"We made it from Harland just in time for the Wish Festival."

"I see. Did you have any trouble passing through the Druidlands?" I glanced at her from the corner of my eye, and saw her stiffen.

"N-No. We mostly tried to avoid the druids, as I heard they are not friendly to outsiders."

"You heard correctly." I scowled. The druids were not even friendly to their own kind. I was still quite new to sensing magic, but I imagined the druids would have felt that whatever magic

Adelaide and Rafe carried was a threat. It was good she had avoided them.

"I was hoping to find...refuge here. But after the events of the last night of the festival..." Adelaide trailed off forlornly, and I nodded sympathetically. "I had no idea the Woman-King had set her sights on this kingdom."

"No one did. Not until it was too late, anyways," I said bitterly.

"The atmosphere here switched from jubilant to dark and oppressed within the span of two weeks." Adelaide shook her head. "It almost feels as if Harland caught up to me."

"Hopefully, her reign will not last long." I sat down on the edge of the next roof and led the way down one of our ladders. At least the tribesmen had yet to find *this* one.

"Where are we?" Adelaide asked as she climbed down behind me. A few moments later, Rafe came limping around the corner and went to stand at her side.

"This is the guild Hyperion, where I work as an herbalist. I can treat Rafe's paw with the supplies in my workshop." I smiled reassuringly before I went up to the door and knocked.

Sirius opened it, and he looked none too happy when he spotted the wolf. He raised one eyebrow at me.

"New patient," I said by way of explanation.

His other eyebrow joined the first, but he opened the door wider to allow the three of us entry.

"If that thing bites anyone..." He let the unspoken warning hang in the air. The wolf wrinkled his snout without showing his teeth, as if he were offended.

"I promise he will behave himself," Adelaide rushed to reassure him, and Sirius gave a curt nod before wandering off.

"This way." I led them back to my workshop, and had Adelaide take a seat while I collected some gauze pads and went about mixing up a healing poultice.

Without needing to be told, Rafe sat as I approached, and placed his paw in my hand when I held it out. I examined the gash he had sustained from the tribesman's dagger, and was relieved to see that the wound was shallow. The wolf hardly even flinched when I applied the cold poultice, but I still wasted no time in securing it in place by wrapping the gauze around it.

"There. Rafe should be right as rain in no time," I declared as I turned to Adelaide. She smiled in relief as I added, "And if you need a place to stay, we have a spare room here. That way, I can change the poultice every day until the wound heals."

"I would appreciate that. Thank you, Astrid." Rafe limped over to me and gave my hand a lick. I tentatively petted his head, surprised at how soft his fur was. I could feel a glimmer of magic in the canine that was both familiar and strange, and I wondered how it was that an animal could possess magic.

"Consider it my thanks for your help earlier. Here, let me show you to your room so you can get settled." I led the pair to a room just down the hall from mine. "Let me know if you need anything."

Adelaide thanked me, and I smiled as I closed the door. I paused outside for a moment, gathering myself, before I slowly approached another door, just down the hall. I raised my hand to knock softly on the wood, but as usual, there was no response.

I turned the doorknob anyway. The curtains were drawn, so the interior was as dark as night. It took my eyes a few moments to adjust to the gloom, and when they did, I could just make out the figure sitting on the room's sole bed, his back to me.

I wilted in disappointment. Orion had been sitting alone in this dark room, staring at the wall every day for the past fortnight. And nothing any of us had said could convince him to come out. It was difficult enough getting him to eat every day, and he hardly spoke unless it was absolutely necessary.

Not that I blamed him—he had been betrayed, and lost both his father and his kingdom in the same night.

But at the same time, I hated seeing him like this. So utterly defeated. My heart ached for him, but none of the words I had offered had seemed to help. Everyone in the guild had tried to offer him comfort, but he still just sat unmoving in the dark, day after day.

I had essentially taken over running the guild in his absence, which I was more than happy to do, but...I missed him. Orion was a shell of his former self, and I felt frustrated by the fact that I had no idea how to help him get better. I spent time visiting him everyday, but it was like talking to a brick wall.

I quietly entered the room and sat on the bed next to him. I let the silence reign for a time, just wanting to let him know that he was not alone in his darkness.

"With help from Nova and Castor, we have perfected the antidote, though I am starting to worry about running out of some of the main ingredients for it. Especially liquid starlight. Yesterday, I had to try substituting stardust instead, which is not quite as effective, unfortunately." I laughed to myself. "I really should have looked into learning how to refine stardust into liquid starlight when I had the chance."

Orion said nothing.

"I cured a husband and wife of the plague today. It seems that only those who publicly protest the new curfews, higher taxes, and influx of tribesmen are stricken with it these days. That tyrant must be purposefully targeting her dissenters now. There are more each time she grants the wish of a tribesman, instead of the wish of an Astorian. Most of the people are still excited, because they believed her promise to grant everyone's wishes. But more and more are finally starting to realize that promise is an empty one." I sighed.

For the first time in weeks, Orion slowly turned his head to look at me. But when he did, his blue eyes looked flat and dull. And when he finally spoke, my heart sank at his words.

"They deserve whatever they get."

Orion

I hardly even noticed when Astrid left my dark hole just as quietly as she had come. I had meant what I said, even if the look on her face had stirred a whisper of emotion in the void in my chest.

The visits of my guild members all blurred together, just as the days did. I knew time was passing with each meal they brought me, but I could not find it in myself to care. The food tasted like ashes on my tongue. And I resented the thrum of starlight I felt that turned my hair silver each night.

I did not want to be cheered up. I did not want to sleep. I did not want to care. I just wanted to sit with the darkness that lived both inside and outside of me. And despite how hard I had tried to keep my secret identity, I could not find it in me to care that the whole guild now knew.

It did not matter. Nothing mattered, not anymore.

And so I sat on the soft bed I could hardly feel and stared at the wall. Whether my eyes were closed or open, I saw the same scene, playing over and over again. I saw the woman I thought I loved, standing over my father's dead body, her iron scimitar red with his blood, with my mother's amulet clutched in her greedy hand.

Despite everything my father had done for his people, all the wishes he had granted, those same people had hardly even protested the usurping of the throne. Where were the countless sick and injured he had healed? Where were the entrepreneurs whose dreams he had turned into reality? Where was the child who had cost my mother her life?

None of them had any sense of gratitude, of loyalty. It seemed none of them cared who was granting their wishes, so long as their wishes continued to be granted.

I curled my lip in disgust. They deserved whatever fresh hell Nyra would visit upon them. They would learn the hard way that unlike my father, Nyra only cared about herself.

Resentment and bitterness wrapped around my throat like a thorny vine, choking me. Was *this* the cruel reward for my parents' sacrifices? Was *this* where their legacy ended?

How dare the world continue on, as if its brightest star had not just been ruthlessly snuffed out!

His last moments replayed in my mind, sending me spiraling once more. I could hardly believe that he was really gone, too. That I was now completely alone.

The blood-stained birthday present my father had given me as he lay dying in my arms sat untouched on the nightstand. I could hardly even bring myself to look at it.

A month ago, I had not believed it possible to resent the day of my birth any more than I already did. How wrong I had been. The day would now forever mark the passing of *both* of my parents. The day I became an orphan.

Someone knocked at the door. I ignored it, as usual. I vaguely wondered why they even bothered to knock, if they were just going to barge in anyways.

"Get up, Sterling," ordered a deep voice. Rigel.

I did not move. My eyes rested comfortably on the wall, and I did not want to move them. I felt like I was floating in water, in the peaceful depths where no one could reach me.

"You are going to get up, and you are going to spar with us," commanded Leo from behind me.

I did not speak. They would give up eventually, and leave me alone with the darkness.

Their footsteps stomped up to the bed. I felt rough hands grab me under the armpits and haul me to my feet, breaking the peaceful trance. I sputtered and thrashed, trying to break their hold.

But their grips were like iron, and they merely grunted at my antics. Astrid and an unfamiliar girl with raven hair watched silently as Leo and Rigel dragged me out of my room and outside to the garden. I felt only a flicker of embarrassment before it winked out.

They threw me onto the grass, the sunlight blinding me after weeks spent in the dark. Leo chucked a wooden practice sword at my chest. I let it hit me, not bothering to catch it. It bounced off my chest and landed on the grass.

"You are going to spar with us, whether you like it or not," Leo declared.

I slowly climbed to my feet, squinting, and turned to walk back into the house. Rigel blocked the way and shoved me back. I glared at him.

"Move."

"You have had plenty of time to mope. It is time you start living again, instead of acting like a living corpse." Rigel glared back at me. "Nyra declared that you are dead, Sterling. Are you going to let your people believe her? Are you going to prove her right?"

For the first time since I woke up after being poisoned, I felt something. An ember of anger flared to life, in stark contrast to the numbness and despair.

"Leave me be," I rasped, with a voice weak from disuse. I went to move around Rigel, but he shoved me back again. The ember grew into a flame.

"Tried that. Look how effective that was," Leo scoffed, gesturing at me. "No, if you are not going to come out of that cave of a room on your own, then we will just have to make you. Pick up the sword."

"I told you to leave me alone!" I croaked, scowling. "And I am not *moping*. I am *grieving*, so leave me be!"

"Sure looks like moping to me," Rigel said.

"My father was murdered!" I yelled hoarsely, my grief turning into a burning rage. Every word they spoke fanned the flames of my anger. Why did they refuse to leave me alone?!

"So was mine!" Rigel's face tightened with pain, but he held my gaze unflinchingly. The flames dimmed.

I looked away first. "I know."

"Not all of us have the *luxury* of wallowing in our pain and ignoring the world. *Some* of us have to carry on, even if we would rather drown in our grief too. Because we have others who *depend* on us. I thought you of all people would understand that," Rigel said softly.

I bristled.

"Giving up on life is *not* the same as grieving. It is time for you to face the world once more," Leo declared.

"The world can burn for all I care," I snarled darkly, the same bloody scene playing on in my mind.

"Would you care if *we* burned?" Rigel asked quietly. "If *Astrid* burned?"

I ground my teeth.

"Yes." I barely moved my lips.

"What was that? I could not hear you!" Leo needled at me.

"Of course I would *care*," I admitted grumpily.

"Are you sure? Because Astrid was nearly captured by a group of tribesmen yesterday, while saving the plague-stricken." Rigel's words cut me to the core, and I snapped my gaze up, a flash of fear replacing the anger and beating back the numbness.

"What?! You let her go alone? Where were you two? Or Noctus and Sirius?" I demanded.

"Where were *you?*" Leo stuck a finger in my chest, but it was the accusation in his tone that hurt me. "While Astrid and the rest of us were risking our necks, you were holed up in your room, staring at the wall."

I clenched my jaw. I had no excuse. Rigel had lost his father too, but *he* was still trying to do what he could.

"Every one of us was either gathering ingredients or delivering antidotes. Even Nova and Castor have had to dodge patrolling tribesmen on their trips. Since *you* stopped caring about anyone but yourself, Astrid and the *rest* of us have had to pick up all the pieces," Rigel explained.

That stung. I opened my mouth to argue, then closed it. They were both right. I just did not want to admit it. Of course Astrid, responsible person that she was, would take over command while I was...wallowing. But to hear that she had very nearly been taken by the people who had already stolen so much from me...

"You are *not* alone, Sterling," Rigel softened his tone. I was startled when he said my name without my title. We had been boys the last time he had done that. "And...I need you to be there for me, too, just as I want to be there for you. I need my brother back."

A lump rose in my throat.

Leo picked up the wooden sword from where it had fallen in the grass. This time, when he tossed it at me, I caught it.

"Focus on the people you have left, not the ones who are already gone. It is fine to miss them, but those who have departed no longer need you—at least, not like your guild members need you." Leo grabbed his own practice sword from where it leaned against the fence, readying it in front of him.

I frowned down at the rough wooden hilt in my hand. Their words had struck a chord in me. My grief still hovered at the edges of my mind, like a great tidal wave threatening to swallow me whole once more. But the thought of losing Astrid, or anyone else in my chosen family, to that treacherous snake and her goons kept the wave at bay.

I refused to lose anyone else to her!

I tightened my grip on the sword and took up my fighting stance. Leo nodded in approval, the fatherliness of that gesture alone almost threatening to send the tidal wave crashing down on me. But I set my jaw, refusing to give in to that temptation.

"Spar with me." I threw his earlier order back in his face.

Rigel and Leo just grinned, and raised their swords in answer.

Astrid

"**W**hy are you buying stardust from the starships instead of from the apothecaries?" Nova asked curiously as we walked.

Adelaide walked behind us, and Rafe trailed at her side, his ears pricked and alert as he watched our surroundings. She had insisted on accompanying me, but I was trying to be careful about exactly how much of the guild's activities I revealed to her. She had been nothing but reliable so far, but I still found myself reluctant to fully trust her. Especially with any information related to Orion's identity. Not after what had happened with Nyra.

"The new taxes have reduced the starships' profits to practically nothing, so they have completely stopped selling to them." I grimaced. "They only sell in secret, now, to avoid their taxes going to support Nyra's regime."

I led the way down a series of increasingly cramped streets as we approached the lake where starships docked. I had taken a rather circuitous route, not wanting to have to lay eyes on the burnt-out shell of Warehouse 13, where Orion and I had confronted Khalifon not once, but twice. I reasoned that taking the long way around would also help us stay under the radar and avoid catching the attention of another patrol.

"What exactly *is* stardust?" Nova asked after a while, scrunching up her face in confusion.

"Stardust is composed of tiny crystals that contain the magic of the stars. Stars constantly emit bits of stardust alongside their starlight, and even a light dusting on a ship will allow it to fly in the sky, just as the stars themselves do," I explained.

"The ships can fly?!" An excited gleam entered Nova's eyes, and I easily anticipated her next question. "Does it work on people, as well?"

"No, for some reason stardust can only make non-living things fly." I tilted my head to the side, thinking. "No one quite knows the reason. I suspect only a fallen star could tell us."

"Oh." Her expression fell. "Do you know how the Astorians discovered that stardust could make objects fly?"

"I believe the late queen and king discovered that fact, during their journey here from Harland. They needed a way to move across a raging river, to escape the witches that were chasing them."

Nova went quiet, her expression souring at the mention of witches. Had she lost her parents to the magic-wielders? Most orphans preferred not to talk about how they had ended up at the orphanage, and it was an unspoken rule not to pry.

"How is stardust collected, then?" Nova's smile seemed a tad forced as she returned to the previous subject.

"Each starship usually has at least one starbird on board. The birds have black feathers, as dark as the night, with white speckles on the undersides of their wings and bellies. Their perfect natural camouflage allows them to blend in with the night sky, making it nearly impossible for their prey to see them coming." I had yet to see one of the birds up close, and they slept during the day, so it was hard to catch a glimpse of one even while trading directly with the captain and crew.

"And these birds collect stardust? Do they have a magical ability, like the sandvipers of the desert?" Nova asked. She had been studying up on them while making antidotes for the plague.

I grimaced at the mention of the source of mirage magic, but continued my explanation. "Starbirds have an almost magnetic pull on stardust and even starlight, which both help enhance their natural camouflage. Because they fly so high while hunting small rodents and other small birds, stardust collects in their feathers, with some of it trailing from their wings as they fly. I have been told it is quite a beautiful sight."

Orion was the one who had initially described them to me. As the prince, it came as no surprise he had been privy to such a sight. My heart ached at the thought of him, and I inwardly winced at the reminder that I had not been the one to finally snap him out of his all-consuming grief. He was still acting rather morose, but at least he no longer sat alone in a dark room all day and night.

"I would certainly like to see one of those birds. Do you suppose the captain we are going to meet today will have one?" Nova pulled me out of my depressing thoughts.

"Likely not." Her expression fell. "Since the birds are difficult to tame, most captains keep a careful watch over them, and never allow a stranger to get too close to them, for fear they may try and steal it."

"I suppose that makes sense." Nova fell silent when I held up my fist, peering around the next corner cautiously to make sure the coast was clear of any patrolling tribesmen. Adelaide and Rafe stopped behind us as well. I hoped she was not too offended that I had turned today's outing into a lesson for my apprentice, but she seemed content to simply listen.

"Adelaide, would you and Rafe mind purchasing a case of glass vials from the warehouse over there?" I gestured to one of the few buildings that still had a lit lantern glowing at its entrance.

"Not at all." She flashed me a quick smile as she accepted the small coin purse I handed her, but I could tell she felt a little put-out.

But part of my agreement with the captain we were about to meet was that no one outside of Hyperion was allowed to know about our little arrangement. Since Nyra was actively looking to punish any disobedient captains, it was better that as few people as possible knew what she and her ship looked like.

I waited until she and Rafe were out of sight before I continued, stepping into the descending twilight and approached the docks. A massive ship was tethered at nearly every one of the berths, their bare masts scratching at the darkening sky. All lay quietly, bobbing in the water, the only noise the lapping of the lakewater at their hulls. The scent of wood and tar suffused the air, and a few gulls circled overhead, riding the warm air currents.

I arrowed straight for one of the mid-size ships that was docked two-thirds of the way down. It was worn but in good repair, and a flag featuring three stars on a dark field flew from the highest mast. Astoria's flag. How brave—or perhaps, foolhardy—of them. Nyra had already burned three ships whose captains refused to replace that flag with hers.

At the end of the dock waited a lone figure. She stood a good hand taller than me, and her rigid posture and muscled frame gave her an imposing aura of authority. She wore a sharp naval jacket with gold pauldrons on the shoulders, and a cutlass hung from her belt, next to her spyglass. Her tall leather boots were practical and well-shined, and her gloves were surprisingly clean. Her dark hair was shot through with gray at the temples, and a scar I had never had the courage to ask about ran from just below one stormy-gray eye to her sharp jawline.

"Captain Jolene!" I called in greeting as we approached.

"How do you know the captain?" Nova sounded impressed.

"I have been one of her best customers for years, so she deals with me directly instead of through her crew," I murmured back.

"Astrid, about time you showed up," she groused, her eyes looking Nova up and down appraisingly.

"It pays to be careful," I said grimly, before making the introductions. "Speaking of, how much are the goods today?" I nodded my chin at the pouch on her belt that was no doubt filled with stardust. It was less full than I had hoped.

I mentally calculated how many antidotes I could make with that, and came up short. Now that I no longer had Orion's wishes to fall back on, all of the desperate hopes of our stricken allies fell on me. And I was feeling the pressure.

"Ten silver," she replied. I tried not to grimace at what was nearly double the price from a few months ago. Our funds were now limited, as well.

"How about nine?" I countered.

She raised an eyebrow. "I will take nine, but no lower. Only the true loyalists dare to do business with me now, so the budget has become increasingly tight."

"Believe me, I understand." I counted out the coins and handed them over, and she passed me the pouch.

"Any liquid starlight today?" I asked hopefully, even knowing what her likely answer would be. It was far more potent, and therefore required much less work on my part.

"'Fraid not." The captain laughed humorlessly. "Hard enough just to catch the stardust these days, without getting caught ourselves."

"Are some of the other starships working for Nyra now?" Nova questioned.

"Aye. And that tyrant is not so keen on sharing the stardust. More captains are succumbing to her extortion every day. Fortunately for me, I have always kept my private affairs close to the chest, so the most she can do is levy fines against me for the flag." She gestured up at the cloth, which was flapping proudly in the breeze.

"I know I do not have to ask, but please do not let her henchmen catch you. She would gladly have your ship burned as well, if you linger too long." My gaze fell on one of the empty berths, where the edges of the wooden dock were charred and blackened.

"Never fear, I am far too quick for that desert snake," Captain Jolene scoffed. "I will send you a starnote once I have collected more stardust for you."

"I would appreciate it. I will buy however much you can collect—and should you or any of the crew be poisoned by the plague, I will provide as many antidotes as you need."

"That would be appreciated," she said guardedly. Although we had been conducting business for years, the captain was extremely cautious—she never allowed anyone but her crew back on her ship.

Under Nyra's tyranny, such tendencies had served her well. And since there were precious few suppliers of stardust left, I was doubly grateful for her caution. Hopefully, I would not have to barter with any of the other, less reputable captains—if they would even be willing to do business with a female. Sailors had bizarre superstitions, but at least Jolene seemed to be largely irreverent of such tales, being a woman herself.

"Until next we meet, then." I gave the captain a smile before turning to leave, and heard her footsteps on the gangplank.

Nova walked in silence beside me until we were back in the shadowy alleys, where we paused to wait for Adelaide and Rafe. They soon arrived, Adelaide holding a new case of glass vials, and we resumed our walk.

"Why is the tribeswoman taking all the stardust?" Nova asked.

I scowled. "She is most likely looking for ways to amass the kind of starpower needed to grant her wish. But I doubt all of the stardust in Astoria would be enough to revive the desert oases." I skirted around mentioning the amulet. It had not been too long since she had joined us, so I decided it was best not to mention any national secrets just yet.

"How much magic would you even need for something of that scale?" Adelaide murmured to herself. Nova nodded in agreement.

"Too much. I doubt even the witches could do such a thing, even if they sacrificed many lives to accomplish it." Both Nova's and Adelaide's expressions melted from curious to blank in a heartbeat. Changing the subject, I asked Adelaide, "In your travels, have you discovered any herbs that may have a similar effect to stardust or starlight? I have started researching alternatives, just in case Nyra commandeers all of the starships in the future."

Adelaide brightened. "Though not quite the same, there *are* a handful of herbs from the mountains that may have similar effects. I have not seen any of them growing here, or being offered for sale in the apothecaries I have visited with you. It may be worthwhile to experiment with them, and I would like to see if combining them with northern herbs might have different effects..."

I smiled to myself as Adelaide rambled on. The three of us, plus Castor, had already spent several evenings working side-by-side in my workshop, and I had learned that once I got Adelaide or Nova talking about herbs and the like, they would keep going on and on for hours if I let them. We were all quite alike in that respect.

I heard her wolf heave a quiet sigh. Despite how the constant stream of noise seemed to bother him, he never left her side. He suddenly lifted his head, and I followed his gaze to a shadowy hint of movement at the edges of my vision. I felt a spike of alarm as the wolf's hackles raised for a moment before lowering again.

A sense of unease fluttered in my stomach, but I tried to push it down. If the tribesmen had spotted us, they would have attempted to capture me, especially if they realized what kind of contraband I carried in the pouch.

Had it simply been someone else passing by, returning home just in time for Nyra's new curfew? Or had it been someone with more sinister intentions?

Just to be safe, I took the long way home.

Orion

I sat on my bed in the dark, unable to bring myself to open the blood-stained birthday present in my hands. My birthday had come and gone, marking the beginning of my eighteenth year. I continued staring blindly at it long after the rest of the guild went to bed for the night.

Absently, I ran my thumb over the wrinkled paper, watching the ribbon bounce slightly from the disturbance. Rigel and Leo's efforts to snap me out of my grief had helped me more than they would ever know, but I still struggled at night. The stars were a constant reminder that both of my parents were gone. I hoped that at least my father truly had reunited with my mother. Were they both watching over me now from above?

This gift must have been important if he had insisted on giving it to me, even in such a nightmarish situation. I was almost afraid to find out why.

Slowly, I pulled on the tail of the ribbon, the blue satin unwinding before it floated to the floor. With stiff but careful fingers, I peeled off the paper and set it aside. A small velvet box sat in my hands, the kind that was usually reserved for jewelry. I slowly opened the lid, and a note fell out onto my bed.

But I nearly forgot about it when I saw what was inside the box. A star-shaped pendant that was translucent like colored glass rested on a bed of crushed velvet. It reminded me of my father's amulet, despite its less polished appearance. I picked it up with trembling fingers, and immediately felt the hum of starlight from within it. Unlike the amulet, however, this pendant felt brittle, as if it would shatter if I dropped it.

I held it up to the moonlight streaming through the window, and gazed in awe at the carved facets that glimmered with a rainbow of colors. A kernel of silver starlight glowed in the very center, so faint it was nearly undetectable. It felt almost identical to the magic of the amulet. I felt a sense of dawning hope. Could it be...?

With trembling fingers, I reached for the folded note that had fallen out, and nearly sobbed when I saw my name written in my father's familiar script. I reverently unfolded the note, and began to read.

My dearest Sterling,

Happy birthday! It feels as if the last eighteen years have passed in the twinkle of a star, but I have treasured every moment.

I may be reluctant to admit it aloud, but I do believe you were right, Sterling. I should have begun teaching you to use the amulet long ago. I simply could not bear the thought of a simple mistake costing me you, too. Which is why, starting tomorrow, your training will begin in earnest. I will be right by your side the entire time, and I promise I will keep you safe as you take this next step forward.

I wanted you to have this pendant. Your mother crafted it for you from a piece of a shooting star, as soon as we realized we were expecting our own little star. Combined with the properties of a shooting star, the starlight magic she poured into it has the power to grant any one wish—but only one, so use it wisely.

I am so proud of you, and of the man you have become. The way you successfully managed this quarter's Wish Festival opened my eyes to how much you truly care for our people. I can rest easy knowing that after I am gone, the Kingdom of the Stars will be in good hands. But of course, I expect to be surrounded by a gaggle of little grandchildren long before then!

I know your mother is just as proud of you as I am.

Love always,

Your father

Silent tears streamed down my face. Bittersweet love tinged with loss and grief rampaged through me, and I felt my magic stir in response, silvering my hair and eyes and sending miniature stars swirling into the air around me. How cruel and wonderful it was, to have known a familial love so profound, only to have it torn from my grasp and the smallest portion of it returned to me in this gift.

I stared longingly out the window at the stars that glimmered beyond my reach, wondering if they missed me nearly as much as I missed them. I closed my fingers around the precious pendant, holding it against my heart. I finally felt the sharp edges of my grief begin to soften.

When I set the box down, I heard a slight scraping noise, and upon closer inspection noticed the starsteel chain. Carefully, I attached the pendant to the necklace chain, and hung it around my neck. It was not the same as the amulet, but I still found its weight comforting, like a hot bath after a long day.

I silently vowed to take better care of this one.

Had I received this gift just a few days before my birthday, I might have considered using its power to revive the oases in the desert. But now...now, I had no desire to use my mother's gift for the sake of the person who had killed my father. I imagined my father had not used it for a similar reason.

I nearly laughed aloud to myself at the notion that had Nyra waited one single, solitary day to stage her coup, I very well might have used my mother's gift for her sake. Then, I would still be wrapped around her little finger, but my father might still be alive.

Too worked up to sleep, I decided to take a walk. I could not bear to sit still one moment longer. Fortunately, the silver starlight had faded, returning my hair and eyes to their normal hues of black and blue. I threw on a long coat and slipped out of the silent guildhouse.

I buried my hands in my pockets as I strolled along, keeping my footsteps light and soundless on the cobblestones. The moon and stars provided plenty of light to see by, but there were few obstacles to watch out for in the silent streets. I glanced up at the stars, almost out of habit, resentment whispering through me once more at the unfairness of it all.

But then I heaved a sigh through my nose. Life was never fair, and I knew that.

My feet took me through the dark and quiet merchant district, and I found myself wandering in the direction of Lake Hesperia. A fresh wave of melancholy hit me at the name: Despite her protests, my father had insisted on naming it after his wife. Even after she ascended, he refused to change it.

It was always the unexpected, little things like that that caught me off guard and gave me a swift punch to the gut.

"Get back here, you brat!"

I jumped to the side as a young girl sprinted past me, something black and fluffy clutched protectively to her chest. An angry tribesman was hot on her heels, his scimitar raised angrily. I instinctively reached for my starsword as the man ran past, cursing when my hand found only empty air. My beloved sword was still in the castle, and I had yet to claim a new one from the spares we kept at the guild.

I joined the chase, my sharp grief fueling my growing fury. I was not about to let a tribesman harm someone right in front of me *again*. And it certainly did not help that this one in particular reminded me of that bastard Tariq.

I pumped my legs faster, my sore muscles screaming at me from the sparring session last morning. I drew up alongside the big man, and just as we raced past the mouth of an alley, I shoved into his shoulder, hard. He went flying into the dark alleyway, and I had to catch myself before I slammed into the wall.

But the girl's footsteps grew fainter up ahead, so I put on another burst of speed to catch up to her. She was dressed in clothes that had been patched together so many times they resembled a quilt, and if I had to guess, I would say that she was a year or two younger than Nova. And by the terrified look she tossed me over her shoulder, she likely thought I was with the tribesman. That irked me to no end.

I recognized the bakery that was coming up on the left, so with one last sprint, I caught up to the slip of a girl, grabbed her around the waist, and hauled her into the alley beside the bakery. She began to scream, so I put a hand over her mouth.

"I knocked that tribesman into an alley, but he will be back in no time. Follow me if you do not want to be caught by that brute." She stopped screaming, watching me with wide, blue eyes. She slowly nodded her head, so I removed my hand and released my hold.

"We keep ladders hidden in many of these alleys, in case we are in need of a quick escape," I explained as I strode to the back and grabbed the ladder, steadying it. "I have found that people rarely look up."

She still seemed nervous, so I decided it would be best to give her a choice. So I scurried up the ladder first and waited at the top to hold it steady. She looked hesitantly between me and the mouth of the alley, but the sound of heavy panting and rapid footsteps approaching made her choice an easy one.

She scrambled up the ladder with one hand, the other still holding tightly to her black bundle. Wait, did the bundle just *move?* When she reached me, I helped her over the edge and pressed down on her back to encourage her to lay flat. We both held our breaths as the tribesman ran past with only a glance at the alley. I waited until he had turned a corner and was out of sight and hearing range before I sat up.

"They have yet to find most of our ladders, so feel free to use them next time." I looked down at the girl, who was still watching me warily. "My name is Orion, by the way. May I ask yours?"

"Aria." Her windswept brown hair fell over one side of her face like a curtain she could hide behind.

"Chee," said the bundle in her arms.

We both looked down in surprise, and I was shocked to see a bird's head emerge from the bundle of what were clearly black feathers, now that I took a closer look. It cocked its head to one side, opening and closing its great wings. My eyes widened when I noticed the flecks of stardust on its feathers, and I took a cautious step back.

"Where on earth did you get a starbird?" I breathed.

"The invaders stole it from a starship. The captain hired me to steal it back." She tried to wrap her thin arms around its wings again, but it jumped into the air and landed on my shoulder, much to both of our horror.

I sighed in resignation as it began to preen my hair, and some of the stardust fell from its wings onto me. My hair began to glow with silvery starlight, and Aria's mouth dropped open in shock.

I tried to remove the bird and hand it back to the girl, but its feathers were slippery, and it would just fly back to its perch on my shoulder. It must have gotten annoyed with me, because it then decided to stand on my head.

"Could you not?" I grumbled at the bird, but it simply clucked at me in response. This had happened the last time I was near a starbird, when my father took me to tour some ships as a boy, but at that time, its stardust had not triggered any sort of reaction. It must have sensed the starlight within me, even when I myself had no clue it was there.

"Why are you glowing?" Aria was gaping at me. Now that I had given up trying to remove it, the large bird of prey hopped back to my shoulder and resumed preening.

"Because of the stardust on this one's wings. Will you keep this a secret for me, Aria?" I asked hopefully.

She looked like she was thinking about it for a minute, but eventually she nodded. "You *did* help me, so I will keep your secret. Can you help me glow too?"

"I am afraid it would be too easy for the invaders to spot you if you went around glowing all the time." She pouted, so I quickly added, "Besides, you would scare your parents half to death if you returned all glowy."

Aria looked down as I ruffled the bird's feathers, and it stretched appreciatively.

"I do not have parents. Not anymore. It was just me and my mother, but the plague took her."

"I...I am sorry to hear that." I inwardly kicked myself. I had nearly forgotten that I was not the only one who had lost a loved one in recent weeks. A lump rose in my throat. "I...lost both of my parents, as well."

Aria finally came closer to me, and placed her hand on my arm for a brief moment. Here I was, supposedly comforting her, but she was trying to console me, instead. For the first time, she gave me a weak smile. "So you hate the invaders too, for bringing the plague?"

"Yes."

"I will share a secret with you, then. The King-Killer said the prince is gone too, but I do not believe her." I blinked in surprise at hearing her speak of me.

"Why?" I asked before I could think better of it.

"Because she is a trickster. And because if he were really gone, too, then she would not need to take all the stardust and this starbird. I think she is planning something, but I know he will not let that happen."

"And you...believe the prince can stop her?" My gut twisted.

"He has to!" Hope and desperation shone in her eyes. "He just has to. Or else...what will happen to us?"

"I..." I trailed off. I had been so consumed by my grief and anger at Nyra and the people who had helped her that I had nearly forgotten all those who had stood by the royal family, all those who had been powerless to stop the tribesmen but had been counting on *me* to do so.

The words I had spoken so callously to Astrid echoed in my ears: *They deserve whatever they get.*

Shame washed over me. Clearly, I had not been wholly abandoned by my people. The girl right in front of me was a shining example. My father had had faith in me, trusting that I would do right by them, and I wanted to live up to his expectations. They had not forsaken me, and I would not forsake them, either.

"I think you are right, Aria." I smiled down at her and ruffled her hair. She beamed up at me, and even the starbird rubbed its face against mine. "Please come to guild Hyperion if you ever need work, or just a safe place to rest. But for tonight, let me walk you back to Lake Hesperia, so you can return this obnoxious little fellow to his ship."

"Thank you, Orion." Aria chatted on as we hopped from rooftop to rooftop, and when the towering masts of the starships filled the horizon, I nudged the starbird back into her arms. This time, it went willingly.

I watched from the rooftop until Aria and the starbird had safely boarded one of the ships, my heart lifting a little when she stopped to wave in my direction before disappearing inside.

As the first rays of dawn banished the darkness and turned the waves to gold, I finally found the resolve that Nyra had shattered so completely. She had taken my mother's amulet. She had taken my father. And she had taken my kingdom.

But I was going to take them back.

Astrid

"A re you certain you want to split up?" Noctus asked again.

"Yes, I will be fine," I reassured him. "I know that area well, and I have not seen many patrols there. The man who requested treatment is one of our top supporters—as well as a vocal dissenter against the new regime. Hence why he has been poisoned. Besides, Adelaide and Rafe will be with me, too."

"We will keep a close eye out for any tribesmen," she promised him. Rafe wagged his tail.

Noctus nodded, though he seemed less confident in them than I, and brandished one of our precious vials of antidote. "Once I have finished seeing to the other patient, I will come to pick you up."

"I would appreciate it. I was hoping to stop by one or two apothecaries afterwards, just to check if they have been able to restock some herbs. With so many of the administrative staff either fled, killed, or imprisoned, trade has practically ground to a halt."

"Understood. But…always keep an eye on your surroundings, just in case," he advised. "If only a certain *someone* could assist us, instead of sleeping the day away…"

"Orion has…been doing much better than a few days ago." I gave him a strained smile. "If we give him a little more time, I am certain he will be back to his old self again."

The hard set of Noctus' mouth softened. "He had better. If Leo and Rigel had not intervened, *I* would have. While I can empathize with him, it was not right of him to leave all of his responsibilities on your shoulders."

"Thanks to everyone in the guild pitching in a bit more, it has been manageable." Though I did miss Orion's reassuring, confident presence, I remembered what a wreck I was in the days after my mother's passing.

"Still…"

"You were not there, Noctus." He flinched, but I continued, "Nyra killed his father while she looked like *him*. She had used sandberries to induce his affections, and when he did not immediately give her what she wanted, she killed his father right in front of him, revealed she had only been using him, and stole his mother's treasure—and almost succeeded in killing him, as well."

I nearly mentioned his kingdom too, but managed to keep that to myself. While most of the guild knew who Orion was,

Adelaide did not. For now, I had every intention of keeping it that way. I could tell Adelaide was curious, but she held her tongue, seeming content not to pry.

Noctus blanched, before looking down. "I did not know the extent of her betrayal."

"We are *all* he has left. After everything he has endured, I think he has earned a little grace." So long as he did not remain locked in his room forever, we could manage on our own for a time. Though my own time was slipping through my fingers like sand.

When Noctus remained silent, I slung my satchel over my shoulder, the muffled clinking of glass reassuring me that even if I had to make a quick escape, the cloths I had wrapped around the glass would keep them from breaking. Their contents were too valuable to waste.

"You should be careful too. Send me a starnote once you are on your way over." He nodded to us both, and I set a hand on his shoulder for a moment before we left the guild house.

Although there were still plenty of people out in the streets, going about their daily errands, the atmosphere was hushed and tense. Children no longer ran laughing through the throngs of people, playing games and making mischief. Now, their mothers kept them close, hushing them for the smallest of noises.

Tribesmen and women strolled boldly through the streets, sneering at the natives, who in turn gave them a wide berth, but still darted dark glares at them when the foreigners' backs were turned.

Many of the wells now lay deserted, as well. Thanks to our efforts, most people now knew the true source of the plague. We had been covertly circulating the news, and the ferocious pace of gossip and word-of-mouth had done the rest, spreading like a wildfire in a dry forest.

I kept my head down to blend in with the afternoon crowd, the distinctive black tips of my hair tucked up in a bun. Fortunately, brown hair was quite common in Astoria, making it easier for me to hide in plain sight. Adelaide was quiet, and even Rafe seemed to sense our need to avoid notice. After passing through the merchant district, we slipped into one of the more affluent neighborhoods, where the houses were large and painted, with decorative flower boxes at the front windowsills.

After a moment of silent debate, I turned to Adelaide. "Would you and Rafe keep watch out here? For tribesmen?" While I was starting to open up to her more and more, I thought it might be safer to wait a little longer before I revealed the identities of some of our most important allies.

Adelaide nodded eagerly. "I will pretend to be pruning the flowers. If I spot any tribesmen behaving strangely, I will have Rafe bark three times to let you know." Then she paused, and frowned as she looked at the exact house down the street that I was about to enter. "But...are you sure this patient is trustworthy?"

I frowned. "What makes you ask that?"

"I just...something feels off."

"My patient has been a loyal customer and supporter of Hyperion for years. No need to worry." I smiled at her reassuringly, but her unease left me feeling unsettled as well.

"If you are certain." She bit her lip. "Rafe and I will be extra vigilant."

"I will be counting on you both." I gave Rafe's head a gentle pat.

Trying to shake off my unease, I went up to the door painted a shade of blue that resembled the sky on a cold winter's morning and rapped the starsteel knocker against the wood. After a moment, the housekeeper answered, and quickly ushered me up to the second floor, where my patient's bedroom was located.

I briefly noted that the maids seemed to be absent today, but reasoned that perhaps they still feared the plague was a contagious disease, and not caused by a liquid poison. Instead of the housekeeper announcing my visit as she had before, she simply knocked on the door and practically fled, her face as drawn as if a phantom were hovering nearby.

My gut twisted. Something felt off here, something beyond just the normal response to the plague.

"Enter," rasped a voice beyond the door.

I took a deep breath before pushing the door open. Mr. Tanner lay on his four-poster bed, the curtains drawn tight over the large windows that looked down on the street below. A single lamp by the bed did a poor job of illuminating the dim interior.

"Mr. Tanner, I am sorry to meet you under such unfortunate circumstances," I said as I approached the bed, trying to ignore my misgivings. "But fear not, for I have an antidote right...here." I withdrew one of the vials from my bag and handed it over. His hand was clammy and shaking.

"Thank you, Astrid, for coming yourself." Mr. Tanner gave a weak cough into his hand, his eyes darting this way and that.

Now that I was closer, I did not see any of the symptoms that usually accompanied the plague. He was certainly pale and clammy, but I detected no bruising or other discoloration on his skin.

"Of course," I said slowly. "You *are* one of our most reliable supporters, after all."

He flinched. "I...I just..." He swallowed convulsively.

"Mr. Tanner? Is something wrong?" My gut was screaming at me now.

Mr. Tanner did not look ill.

He looked afraid.

His eyes darted to the shadows behind me. "Please forgive me."

"Hello, little rabbit."

A heavy hand clamped down on my wrist, and I gave an involuntary scream. My bow and quiver were forcibly ripped from my back as the air shivered next to me and the hidden tribesman discarded his mirage. Behind him, two more tribesmen materialized out of thin air, smug grins of triumph on their faces. My heart began to pound in my ears, even as it dropped to my toes.

My gaze snapped to Mr. Tanner's, but he refused to meet my stare. He had tricked me. He had never been sick with the plague. The whole thing had been an excuse to get me here, a ruse.

No, a trap.

Adelaide had been right. I should have listened to her—I should have trusted her.

No wonder all the maids were gone and the housekeeper was as white as a sheet. They were all terrified of these hulking desert men and their scimitars.

"How? How could you betray us?" I fought wildly against the tears that pricked the back of my eyes, and the wild magic that stirred in response. My heart ached, both the curse and the betrayal taking their toll. "I saved your son!"

"They poisoned him." Mr. Tanner's miserable eyes finally found mine. "They promised me the antidote."

"And thanks to your cooperation, he will be cured—probably," snickered one. Mr. Tanner looked as if he were about to pass out.

"You desert snakes disgust me," I spat, trying to mask my fear with bravado.

The man's grip tightened painfully. "It is a good thing for you my lover wants you *alive*. Though uninjured was never specified."

Thinking fast, I went limp, pretending to be cowed by the brute's threats. The moment his grip eased, I stepped forward and swung my foot upwards where his legs met. The tribesman hunched over in pain, releasing me. One of the others rushed to block the door while the other bent to check on his wounded leader.

But I managed to surprise them.

Instead of heading for the room's sole door, I darted over to the windows. I ripped away the thick curtain with one hand, while the other grabbed a heavy, decorative vase and catapulted it into the window. The glass shattered into thousands of pieces, large chunks and tiny splinters raining down onto the cobblestones below.

Heavy footsteps thundered behind me.

Not bothering to avoid the jagged edges, I leaped for the opening. For an instant, my eyes met Adelaide's, and I thought I would make it. Before I could plunge down to the street below, I was yanked back through the window by the scruff of my tunic and thrown to the ground.

The wind knocked out of me, I lay there with my mouth gaping open like a fish, desperately trying to suck down some air. Before I could even take a breath, a boot slammed into my ribs, sending a bolt of pain through my side. Instinctively, I curled up in a ball, despite the glass that dug into my skin. Finally, I greedily gulped down lungfuls of air, despite the throbbing in my side.

My scalp screamed in pain as I was dragged upright by the roots of my hair. Through squinted eyes, I marked my target, and before they could search me, I unsheathed my hidden dagger and struck out wildly behind me. I staggered as the pressure on my scalp was finally released. The one who had grabbed me cradled his bloodied arm against his chest, cursing up a storm and glaring at me with such hatred that I took a step back.

I leveled my weapon before me as I slowly backed up towards the window. When the other two rushed at me, I slashed in a wide arc, but only managed to nick them. As they retreated, the big one lunged in, backhanding me across the face before I could bring my dagger up.

I cried out as stars burst across my vision, and clung desperately onto the thick curtain to keep from falling onto the sharp glass edges of the window. The world spun around me, my number of opponents doubling, and I vaguely wondered if that was mirage magic or the shock of the blow making me see things. Distantly, I heard the sound of Mr. Tanner sobbing quietly in the corner.

I was a healer, not a fighter. Oh, when would Adelaide or Noctus arrive? Or would there be nothing but bloodied, broken glass to mark my abduction by the time they got here?

Left with little choice, I reached for my wild magic. With only one decorative plant in the room, I had no clue how I could possibly defend myself, but there had to be *something* I could do. Some distraction, some trick...*anything* to buy me some time.

I braced myself for the backlash from the curse I knew was coming.

An instant before I set my magic loose, I heard his pounding footsteps on the stairs. Seconds later, the door was kicked in, and I sagged in relief. Noctus took one look at me, and his normally calm demeanor cracked, his face darkening with rage. In a spray of blood and darkness, the two henchmen went down, their heavy bodies thudding against the polished hardwood floor.

Adelaide and Rafe flew into the room after him. Rafe lunged at one of the men, who had begun struggling to his feet. The two went down in a cacophony of growls and grunts of pain. Adelaide rushed over to me, her hands steady as she helped support my weight.

Starsteel clashed against iron as the lead tribesmen brought up his guard just in time to stop Noctus' strike. Sparks flew from their blades as they danced around the room, his throwing knives making little impact on the big man. They stuck out of his beefy arms and chest like the quills of a porcupine.

I bit my lip as I watched, worried for Noctus. His specialty was in quick strikes from the shadows, not drawn-out, one-on-one battles like this. I swayed on my feet, fighting against the darkness that had begun to lick at the edges of my vision. He must have hit me harder than I thought.

Noctus sliced at his neck, but his short sword screeched against the tribesman's blade as he parried. If I could just give Noctus one single opening...

I watched carefully, and Adelaide helped me creep closer to await our chance. I drew my dagger and handed it to her. My friend's eyes flicked to me, and he began to angle himself so that his opponent's back was to us with a flurry of quick jabs. Adelaide leaned me against the wall and snuck closer, and then darted forward, driving my dagger home into the brute's wide back. He roared in pain and surprise, which was all the opportunity Noctus needed to finish the job.

Adelaide staggered back, and I sagged with relief as the adrenaline faded, and my fresh wounds made known their presence. Noctus rushed over to catch me before I collapsed, his face grim.

"Took you long enough," I rasped.

"Sorry. You know how the old lady likes to chat." Then he grudgingly nodded to Rafe and Adelaide. "Thank them for coming to get me."

Noctus scooped me up into his arms, and I was too weak to protest. He headed for the door-which was now barely hanging onto the frame by its hinges, and glared at the cowering Mr. Tanner.

"We will have words," he ground out, and the man flinched.

Then Noctus swept out of the room, down the stairs, and out the front door, with Adelaide and Rafe trailing worriedly behind. We drew plenty of stares, and even though Noctus was shy of crowds and attention, he glowered boldly at anyone who came too close. He took the main streets until we could dive into the alleys and make our way back to the guild house.

When Sirius opened the door, he blanched and immediately started yelling for Nova and Castor. My two apprentices came running, and trailed behind Noctus as he carried me into one of the patient rooms and set me gently on the bed before hurrying out again.

"What happened?" Nova demanded, putting a hand to her mouth.

"It was a trap," I mumbled. It felt like one side of my lips were swollen. I gently prodded the left side of my face, and winced at the answering pain and swelling I found. I would have wagered my eye was turning an atrocious shade of purple right about now.

Castor rushed over to me and began to examine me for injuries, so I pointed him to my side. "I think he either fractured or broke some of my ribs. I need you to make a couple of poultices and get me a cool rag for my face."

"Of course. I will make the poultices, and Nova will get the rag." My apprentices jumped into action, and I smiled at them proudly, even though it hurt. Once I was gone, these two would be my legacy.

Orion stormed into the room, with Noctus, Sirius and Leo trailing behind. He marched right up to me, and I slowly turned towards him. His face was hard but his hands were gentle as he cupped my face.

His blue eyes swept over my injuries, a storm brewing behind them. Butterflies took flight in my stomach. This was the most emotion he had shown since that night, and he was showing it for me. It almost seemed like he was back to his old self again.

"Who did this to you?" he growled.

"The tribesmen blackmailed Mr. Tanner. The request was a trap," I explained haltingly.

His face darkened even further, and I could feel a tremor go through his hands. "You are not allowed to leave me too." His tone was part order and part desperate plea.

My lips parted in surprise, even as my heart ached. I almost told him the truth right then and there, but the words were stuck in my throat. Instead, I closed my eyes, and leaned into his touch. Despite my best efforts, a tear escaped and cut a cool trail through the fiery pain in my cheek.

"I missed you," I murmured in lieu of a promise.

"Leo, you stay here and guard her. Have Adelaide and the apprentices tend to her. Noctus, Sirius, go and get Rigel. And then get your weapons."

Orion

I clenched and unclenched my hands, the phantom feel of Astrid's tear on my skin driving me mad. I could not recall the last time I had seen her cry. I closed my eyes as I silently berated myself, but the image of her bruised and swollen face haunted me.

I nearly lost Astrid today.

She was *always* there for me, but I had not been there for her. I had been too wrapped up in *myself.*

"Here." I opened my eyes to see Rigel had returned, with Noctus and Sirius flanking him, and the knight was holding out my own sheathed starsteel sword to me, the one I thought had been left in the castle. "At great risk to himself, one of my men smuggled it out. We are not yet bereft of hidden allies within the castle."

A lump rose in my throat. "Thank you."

I took my starsword and attached it to my hip, its familiar weight soothing my soul.

"I promised him a promotion when all of this is over." Rigel's steely eyes met mine, a challenge in their depths. "Are you going to let her take anything—or anyone—else from us?"

I winced internally. I deserved that. I took a steadying breath and set my jaw.

"No. And we are going to start with the tribesmen who nearly took Astrid." Rigel nodded approvingly, and I looked at Noctus. "Lead us to them."

He inclined his head as a show of respect, to his sovereign, and not just his guild master. I had never quite known what I would do about the guild when I eventually became king—I had mostly considered naming a successor and quietly withdrawing from my second home. For the first time, I wondered if it would not be such a bad idea to incorporate my guild, my people, under the royal banner, in an official capacity. Back when I had secrets to keep, that had been only a passing fancy. But now...

Noctus led the way out of the guild house and through the quiet cobblestone streets. The few people still about took one look at us and stepped aside, averting their gazes until we passed. I found myself almost hoping for one of Nyra's cursed patrols to crop up in front of me. I was itching for a fight.

As we sped through the once bright and lively streets of my kingdom, it really hit me just how much it had changed in such a short span of time. A hostile wariness had replaced the easy, cheerful atmosphere, and few people left their homes unless it was absolutely necessary. There were no children playing in the streets, no bands striking up a spontaneous tune. Only grim adults going about their errands, keeping their heads down whenever they spotted someone else.

A part of me felt a spiteful triumph at the clear results of good men standing aside as Nyra took over. But the other part simply felt sad and guilty that I had allowed this to happen, despite my best efforts.

I silently swore to myself that someday soon, I would return the light and laughter to this kingdom.

I knew we had arrived at our destination when I spotted fragments of broken glass glittering under the light of the afternoon sun. I gazed up at the lavishly-decorated home, one I had visited before as a guest for an evening of fine dining and idle chatter. My simmering anger came to a boil when I imagined exactly what had taken place here not twenty minutes ago. Based on the cacophony of yelling and cursing coming from within, the bastards who had dared to lay a hand on my healer were still inside.

Good.

I drew my sword from its sheath. Noctus silently stepped aside, falling in behind me as I kicked open the already-damaged door. The house went silent for an instant, as if holding its breath, before heavy footsteps pounded down the carpeted stairwell. When the first tribesman reached the landing, he froze when he spotted me, before his ugly mug broke out in a twisted grin.

"And here I thought that elaborate trap went to waste. But so long as I return with *you*, I have no need of the girl." He unsheathed his scimitar and leaped down from the landing, raising his weapon high overhead.

"I will not fall so easily!"

I lunged forward to meet him, surprising him, and deflected his blade to the side. It bit into the decorative wooden paneling, and he barely yanked it out in time to defend against my thrust. The screech of metal meeting metal filled the air, and despite the danger, I found myself almost giddy.

It felt good to have my weapon back in my hand again.

I pressed my advantage, forcing the big man back a step. I swung my weapon around in an arc, the blade singing through the air. My opponent grunted from the force of the blow, and I could see the shockwave shudder through the iron and into his arm.

But I felt no pity for him.

He recovered more quickly than I anticipated and swung at my head. I danced backwards, holding a hand up when I saw Rigel move in closer. This was *my* fight.

I charged forward and parried the tribesman's thrust. Beads of sweat formed on my skin, but it was my opponent who was beginning to look rather winded. I grinned, then delivered a brutal flurry of blows that he struggled to parry. A few got through his guard, leaving red lines on his exposed skin.

I glanced up as two more tribesmen hobbled down the stairs, unsurprised when they rushed towards our battle. Rigel and

Sirius surged forward to meet them, Noctus hanging back in reserve, and I brought up my guard just in time to block another strike.

"What a foolish boy. But then, we already knew that." The tribesman grinned at me, and I wondered fleetingly if he had been in the room when my father was killed.

Silently, I berated myself for that lapse in focus. I eyed the iron blade, noting the green sheen of poison coating it that was barely visible in the low light. I shuddered involuntarily at the memories that poison conjured, welcoming the rush of fear and rage it brought.

"Only an unskilled coward would hide behind poison," I hissed back at him.

Never again would I present a desert tribesman or woman the chance to cut me with a poisoned blade.

With a yell, I locked our blades and shoved the mountainous man backwards, trapping him in the corner of the room. I knocked his weapon aside, his confident smirk going with it, and plunged my blade into his chest. He gave one final gasp of disbelief before he went limp.

My chest heaved as I fought for air, my muscles sore after the idle weeks I had spent recovering. This marked my first strike against Nyra since that dreadful night. The first of many.

I ripped the starsword free as I whirled to help my men engage the other two, only to find that they had both handily finished off their opponents as well.

"Good job." I nodded to Rigel and Sirius.

"Noctus did most of the heavy lifting. We simply finished them off after the thrashing he gave them earlier," Sirius replied.

A ghost of a grim smile played on Noctus' lips. "Shall we see what Mr. Tanner has to say for himself?"

At my nod, Noctus led the way up the stairs the tribesmen had just descended, a terrified maid scurrying out of our way as we went. We found the richly-dressed man cowering in a corner of his own bedroom, a familiar glass vial clutched in one white-knuckled fist.

Red tinged my vision at the thought that this sniveling man had nearly cost me Astrid. The fact that we had supported each other only made the betrayal all the worse.

I strode right up to the man and lifted him off the ground by his tunic. He went pale at the look on my face.

"O-Orion, now w-wait a minute," he stammered out. Sweat dripped from his forehead, and the hands he wrapped around the arm holding him aloft were cold and clammy. "It was not my choice t-to—"

"What in the blazing stars did the usurper offer you that was worth the life of my healer?" I growled, twisting the fabric until he started to gasp for breath. Rigel stepped forward, as if to stop me, but I froze him with a look. Still, I loosened my grip.

"The life of my son. They poisoned him." Tears misted his eyes, dripping freely down his face. "Please understand—he is all that I have left!"

"And you trusted them to save him?"

He looked down. "What else could I have done?"

I opened my fist and let the fool fall to the floor. I pointed at the vial he still clutched. "You are holding the antidote."

Mr. Tanner looked at the vial, frowning. "No, this is for the plague, not their poison." He looked back to me, his face going even paler as the truth slowly dawned on him. "No."

"Yes. The plague is a watered-down version of their poison. Had you simply come to us, we would have given you the stronger antidote we prepared."

"How-how do you know if it works?" He was grasping at straws, trying to find a reasonable excuse.

"We know it works because *I* am still breathing." I let that sink in.

Mr. Tanner slowly uncurled his fist, looking at the vial as if it were a snake about to bite him.

"Did they take your son to the castle, or is he still in your home?" Sirius asked quietly.

"He is h-here, in his room." The merchant slowly turned his eyes to Sirius.

"Then touch as much starsteel as you can find to his skin and feed him that potion." Sirius' voice was not gentle, but it was not unkind, either. "If he still suffers, then call on Astrid and ask for a stronger antidote. Whether she responds, however, is entirely up to her."

Shame flitted across his features, but hope shone in his eyes as well. I ran a hand through my hair, blowing out a heavy sigh.

"Well? What are you waiting for?" I asked. "Go tend to your son!"

He scrambled to his feet as suddenly as if he had been struck by lightning, but paused at the door. "And what do I tell the tribesmen who will come knocking?"

"That their trap failed because the girl was not alone," Noctus answered. "Tell them that Astrid will always be under guard now."

Mr. Tanner nodded before he ran out the door and down the hall, calling for his servants to grab hold of everything made of starsteel. I left him to it and led the way back down the stairs and past the bodies, not sparing them a second glance.

The walk back to the guild was a silent one. I wrestled with my tumultuous thoughts and emotions, considering what would come next. It was clear to me that Nyra would continue waging her secret crusade against my guild, targeting those closest to me until I was alone and undefended. Her aim was likely to kill me quietly, to prevent me from rallying the people to rebellion or from being used as a martyr.

Which meant no one connected to me would be safe.

She had proven today how easily she could get to those I had trusted, how even my staunchest supporters could be used against me. And she had shown *exactly* how low she would go to achieve that. Not that her methods surprised me. I had expected as much.

The only way to keep the people I loved safe was to take back the throne and evict the tribespeople who had taken root in my kingdom like thorny, choking weeds.

I rested my hand on the hilt of my sword as I strengthened my resolve. The time for grieving had passed. Now was the time for action.

But revealing that I was still alive to the people *now,* before I had time to prepare, would only cause unrest and needless deaths. No, I would reveal the truth only once I had a solid plan.

"What next?" Rigel asked, as we paused just outside of the guild.

"Next, we go on the offensive. Peace is no longer an option." But then I paused, and looked at each man in turn. "Noctus, Sirius, this was never your fight to begin with. If you choose to leave, I will not think any less of you."

"I pledged myself to Orion, to help you save more people the way you saved my sister. As saving people from a tyrant is an extension of that vow, I will also pledge myself to Prince Sterling." Sirius drew his sword and planted the tip in the ground, kneeling behind it.

"I have known who you were from the beginning," Noctus admitted slowly. "And I will follow where you lead, regardless of where that may be, or the name you go by." He also knelt before me.

"Prince Sterling, allow me to serve you as my father served yours." Rigel followed suit, touching his forehead to the sword he held in front of him.

A lump rose in my throat at the sight. I unsheathed my starsword and lightly tapped each of their shoulders. "Rise, as Knights of Astoria, and my brothers-in-arms. The fight ahead will not be an easy one, but your courage will make it bearable. For though darkness falls..."

"Still the stars find their way," the trio answered as they rose.

"So, how shall we depose a tyrant?" Sirius asked after a moment with a lop-sided grin.

"First, we find some allies. And then, we strike."

Astrid

I heard the creaking of the front door, and the murmur of low, male voices. Orion and the others must be back! I started to rise from the bed before a sudden throb of pain froze the breath in my lungs, and I fell back to the pillows, wincing. I watched numbly as the black crept an inch higher up my hair, devouring the brown coloring.

"You know better than to move suddenly like that," Nova scolded me gently, misunderstanding the source of my pain. Her hands fluttered around my side and my face, checking to see if the movement had loosened any of the bandages.

I chuckled weakly at her expression, once I could breathe freely again. It felt strange to be fussed over by my apprentices like this. Not that it was an entirely unpleasant feeling.

"Can you ask Orion to come to me, then?" I requested, as Adelaide walked in holding a freshly-made remedy, Rafe glued to her side like a shadow.

"Fine, but that remedy had better be gone by the time I get back." The little teasing smile she gave me told me she was enjoying the reversal of our usual roles.

"Yes, mother." I gave a mock huff of annoyance, as Nova used to do, and she rewarded me with a laugh as she slipped out of the room. It had surprised me how much my injuries had shaken both Nova and Castor, but knowing how much they cared about me had warmed my heart as much as it scared me.

How would they take it when the curse ran its course? I glanced at Adelaide as she sat down on the bed beside me. Perhaps they could find a new teacher in her.

"I added some honey to mask the bitterness," she said as she handed it to me.

"Thank you." I had quickly discovered that Adelaide's concoctions never accounted for taste, but I appreciated that she was trying to make her creations more palatable. Still, I hesitated for a moment, and Rafe rested his head on my leg, as if in silent encouragement.

I smiled and downed the whole remedy in one gulp, trying not to breathe through my nose as I did so. The honey definitely helped, but the bitterness still lingered at the back of my throat. Well, hopefully that meant it would be quite potent.

"I mixed in some white willow bark, which should help with the swelling and the pain. I was surprised how few apothecaries here stock it—it seems its healing properties are not as widely known as I believed." Adelaide idly brushed her raven hair over her shoulder, the dark strands reflecting deep purples and indigos.

How I envied her healthy hair.

"Astrid, how are you feeling?" Orion asked as he entered. Nova winked at me from behind him before making herself scarce. The girl was almost too clever that way. "And thank you for tending to her, Adelaide." She bobbed her head.

"Better," I lied, as I scanned him for injuries. I spied smears of blood on his clothes, but no visible open wounds. "Were you hurt? What did you...?"

"Those tribesmen who hurt you will never trouble us again." His blue eyes dimmed with an almost resigned determination.

"Does that mean...?" I trailed off, hoping Orion had finally decided to take action.

"Nyra's days on that throne are numbered," he growled, a familiar spark reigniting in his cold eyes. Still, a part of me wondered if he would be able to do what needed to be done when the time came. Perhaps I should look into some herbs that could counter the effects of sandberries, just in case.

"Adelaide, please pack your things and assist Astrid with hers as well." Orion cautiously held out a hand for Rafe to sniff before patting the wolf on the head.

"Wait, pack? Why are we packing?" Alarm shot through me. Astoria was my home, even as dangerous as it had become over the last few weeks. Orion could not possibly be thinking of sending me away, could he?

"Today has shown me that Astoria is no longer safe for anyone associated with me. And I refuse to lose anyone else I care about." His eyes took on that distant look I had grown to abhor.

"Orion, you cannot just run away from your problems and abandon your people—you are their prince and the only hope they have left!" I exclaimed heatedly, struggling to rise.

"Prince Sterling?" Adelaide gasped quietly beside me, and even the wolf raised his head. I surprised myself with the admission, but I realized that I had grown to trust Adelaide completely after she had helped save me, not once, but twice. Besides, she deserved to know what she risked by staying with us.

"I am *not* running." Orion set a hand on my shoulder reassuringly, pushing me gently back against the pile of pillows. "I am going to seek allies. While I do, I am sending Estelle, your apprentices, and the other non-combatants to a home in Delphini that only my father and I knew about."

"I certainly hope you are not thinking of sending me," I protested hotly. I was determined to stay by his side for however much time I had left, not hidden away in some royal lake house.

"*No.* No, Nyra has already demonstrated that you are one of her top targets. I want you with me at all times, so I can keep you safe." His words sent a thrill through me, and I felt my cheeks grow warm.

"Or me," added Adelaide. There was a breathiness to her voice that sounded almost desperate. "I can do you much more good by your side than tucked away in a secret location. Besides, who will tend to Astrid if her apprentices are not present?"

"I *am* grateful you were there with Astrid today." Orion paused, considering, then finally nodded. "You make a good point. If you are willing to face the dangers alongside us, it would put my mind at ease knowing you are taking care of her while she recovers."

Adelaide let out a nearly silent sigh of relief, and I wondered why she seemed so keen to rush into danger. Perhaps she simply did not want to be left behind. I could understand that.

"I will do whatever I can to help you secure more allies in this fight," I promised him. He gave me a soft smile that set butterflies loose in my stomach.

"I will be counting on you both. I fully intend to reclaim my kingdom and my father's legacy from those desert usurpers," Orion, or rather, Prince Sterling declared.

"I am glad to hear it. Do you intend to seek an alliance with Harland?" I asked.

Neither the desert Tribes nor the druids would ally with us; the witches could perhaps be commissioned for a specific objective, but they typically demanded human sacrifices in exchange for their services. Orion would never agree to such a horrific price.

That left Harland as the only viable ally left on the continent. While Astorians generally looked down upon the practice of slavery and the strict caste system they enforced, Astoria had never fought with the mining kingdom as far as I knew.

But if their forces were composed of slaves and conscripts, could we really accept that sort of aid with a clear conscience?

"No." I blinked, surprised. "I will seek an alliance with the Druid King."

It felt like a bucket of ice water had been upended over my head, dousing the warm excitement from mere moments ago. I had just agreed to accompany Orion to my homeland, to the very place my mother had sacrificed everything to escape. My stomach bottomed out as I faced the spectre of my now very near ending.

What if I came face-to-face with the grandfather who had cast the curse on my mother and I, the one that was even now corrupting my magic and stealing my lifeforce? Would he finish what his curse had started?

I had the horrible feeling that if I went in, I would never make it out of the Druidlands alive.

Orion

"I am counting on you," I said as I gripped Rigel's arm.

"And I, you," he replied solemnly. "Make sure to return unharmed—and with as many reinforcements as you can muster."

I nodded, the small group behind me doing the same. Only Astrid, Leo, Noctus, and Adelaide and her wolf would be coming with me on this dangerous mission. I had charged Sirius with seeing the others to safety—despite their loud protests. Only Rigel would remain behind, to coordinate those still loyal to me both within and without the castle.

"Keep them safe," I ordered Sirius. He inclined his head, and I knew I had nothing to fear.

At least I would have some peace of mind, knowing that Nyra would not be able to go after my guild members while I was gone.

I took one final look around the inn-turned-guildhouse, hoping it would not be the last time I saw it.

"Though darkness falls..." I said quietly.

"Still the stars find their way," they replied softly.

And with that, I turned on my heel and left my second home behind. Leo and Noctus took up position at the back of our little party as we slipped through the quiet streets, with only the crescent moon and some faint starlight to guide us. We kept the hoods of our cloaks pulled down low, and darted from shadow to shadow through the merchant district.

No one spoke; only the faint scuff of boots on stone and the click of Rafe's claws broke the silence of the deep night. Once we made it past the darkened shop windows, I led the way through a quiet neighborhood, my ears straining for the slightest sound. I knew few patrols were out this late, but it never hurt to be cautious.

But as we left the neighborhood and entered the wharf district around Lake Hesperia, Rafe let out a low growl. My heart began to pound, but I quickly scanned our surroundings and ushered the group down the nearest alley, so we could huddle behind a large stack of crates that stank of fish. I kept Astrid behind me and rested my hand on the hilt of my starsword as I finally heard the footsteps Rafe had alerted us to.

We held our breaths as the heavy footsteps drew closer, and I forgot to breathe entirely when they stopped at the mouth of the alley. Had we been spotted?

"Are these patrols truly necessary? These northerners are all so timid and weak," complained one of the tribesmen.

"They may *seem* quiet, but they are a sly bunch. We cannot let our guards down in the midst of enemy territory." I heard the faint sound of fabric rustling, as if the man were stretching

"Why not use a mirage to look like a northerner? That would make things easier," yawned the first one.

"Shhh." It sounded like the second one cuffed the first. "The Woman-King wants to keep our magic a secret until the time is right."

"How long must we wait til then?" grumbled the first, as they both resumed patrolling.

I frowned, feeling uneasy. What more could Nyra possibly have up her sleeve? She already had both the kingdom and the amulet in the palm of her hand. Hopefully, Rigel could find out the reason through his spies before we returned.

I waited until I could no longer hear their footsteps before I signaled the others, and carefully crept out from behind our hiding place. I glanced up and down the road, and when I was satisfied no alerts were being called, continued our flight towards the lake.

My eyes were inevitably drawn to the burned-out husk of Warehouse 13. Astrid slipped her hand in mine, and I gave it a reassuring squeeze. We had defeated that tribesman; now we just had to take down the rest of them. Piece of cake. I tamped down on the humorless laugh that tried to work its way out of my throat.

I had to focus on the things I could control, the things I could change. Starting with myself. I would just have to have faith that the rest would work itself out, somehow.

Wrenching my gaze away from the warehouse, where everything had nearly ended and then begun anew, I skirted around the other hulking storehouses until the docks came into view. Only a handful of starships bobbed on the gentle waves, the faint moonlight silvering the water and the ships' rigging. A hint of brine hung in the misty air, and I suppressed a shiver as I looked at the imposing silhouettes before me.

I glanced up at the sprinkling of stars I could see. *Stars, give me courage.* Perhaps I imagined it, but I could have sworn one of them twinkled at me.

"Which one did you commission?" I asked Noctus in a low tone.

"The *StarSeeker,* a brigantine. She lies just behind the closest galleon," he answered, pointing to one of the docked ships.

As we made our way over to it, I asked, "And you are positive her loyalty lies with us?" Nyra had already shown she was no stranger to setting traps. Once we were on board and in the air, we would essentially be trapped until we landed once more.

"Absolutely. This ship in particular turned pirate in an effort to defy Nyra's new tariffs and fixed prices. Captain Jolene refused to sell her stardust to her, and has been a target ever since." Noctus' tone was firm.

"I would have done the same." I saw little movement on the deck of the *StarSeeker* as we approached, but her sails were lowered and her flags flying.

Ready to set sail.

And hopefully, to carry us to the Druidlands.

I stepped into the brigantine's shadow and approached the gangplank. The moment I set foot on the worn wood, a figure appeared on the deck, motioning for us to board. After exchanging glances with Noctus, I led the way onto the ship.

As I neared, I was able to make out more details. The woman before me was short of stature, but the cutlass at her hip dispelled any conception of frailty. She wore a blue captain's coat with a matching tri-corner hat, and sturdy trousers and boots, with a red sash tied around her waist. Her dark hair was streaked with silver at the temples, and her sun-kissed skin bore lines around her stern mouth and at the corners of her piercing emerald eyes.

"Captain Jolene, I presume?" I glanced around the deck, noting the many crew members who lingered in the shadows. They behaved much like my own master of information. But to my surprise, it appeared to be an all-female crew.

"In the flesh." Her voice was rich and warm, but with a rough edge to it, the kind I imagined could be heard over the roar of the winds and the waves.

Leo inched closer to my side, his gaze riveted to the captain. He stood a full head and a half taller than her, and I got the distinct impression of a war hound approaching a feisty kitten.

"Partial payment upfront." The captain held out her hand expectantly.

"Here you are, my lady," the grizzled soldier said as he gently deposited a coin pouch in her hand, his calloused fingers lingering a heartbeat longer than necessary. The captain's lips parted in bewilderment, and were we in a less dire situation, I might have laughed. I imagined few people called this particular sailor a 'lady.'

I fidgeted anxiously, feeling exposed on the deck. My gaze swept the docks, and fortunately detected no movement. But every moment we delayed was another moment of risk.

"That is *Captain* Jolene to you," she barked back at him, but Leo simply smiled. "I will have no disrespect on my ship—" She stopped abruptly to stare open-mouthed at me.

"There they are!" came a sudden cry.

"Do not let them get away!"

"For the Woman-King!"

Our heads snapped towards the three patrols of tribesmen that had seemingly materialized out of thin air. They were running towards the ship from the other side of the wharf, blades drawn and ready. How had they possibly spotted us from so far away?

"Orion, your hair!" Astrid cried.

She lunged forward and placed some kind of garment over my head, and I realized with dawning horror that my hair had begun to glow. The tribesmen must have seen it! But it was long past the midnight hour! Unless...had my anxiety triggered the change?

"All hands, raise anchor!" the captain hollered. To us, she said, "And I will deal with *you* later."

The crew jumped into action, scurrying across the deck to raise the gangplank and the anchor. The thick chains groaned as the anchor was raised, and with nothing to hold it in place, the full sails began to move the ship away from the dock. Fortunately, the wind was cooperating, but I was worried it would not be fast enough, as the tribesmen were quickly approaching.

Astrid nocked her bow, and Rafe began to growl menacingly. Just as the ship pulled away from the dock, the lead tribesman leaped onto the ladder built into the side of the ship and began to climb. But before Astrid could loose her arrow, Leo rushed forward, and sent the invader plummeting into the calm waters with a single stroke of his sword.

"Now!" the captain shouted.

As one, a crew member at the bow, at the stern and up in the crow's nest reached into the pouches at their waists and scattered stardust onto the wood and the sails. As the ship picked up speed, the wood rattled and groaned. It began to glow as the crew continued throwing stardust onto it, and with one great heave that sent us staggering, the starship lifted from the waves and ascended into the sky.

Astrid

I breathed out a sigh of relief as the *StarSeeker* rose out of range of the tribesmen below, though I could still hear them shouting orders, threats, and curses in equal measure. But my relief was short-lived. The slither of steel cutlasses being pulled from their sheaths filled the cold night air as the crew turned on us with weapons drawn.

We were surrounded, trapped on a floating hunk of wood far above the ground. I tried to tamp down on my rising panic as my hand drifted towards my concealed dagger, and my cursed magic stirred in response to my heightened emotions.

Noctus and Leo turned to face the crew, weapons at the ready, but we were sorely outnumbered.

"How convenient that three patrols just *happened* to be nearby when you gave away our position," Captain Jolene drawled, her own cutlass leveled at Orion. "Which one of you is the witch?"

I felt more than saw Adelaide go still beside me, and Rafe raised his hackles as he moved closer to her. It took me a moment to realize she was referring to Orion's still-glowing hair, and it dawned on me that she believed we had signaled the tribesmen purposefully.

"No one here is a witch," Orion said tightly, before gesturing at his hair. "You are seeing the remnants of star magic, for which I must apologize."

"Star magic?" she scoffed. "You expect me to believe that, when only the king, stars bless his soul, could use it? No, I think this is some trick of the tyrant's."

"You seem to be forgetting that those brutes were aiming to capture *us,* not just *you.* And if we were trying to signal them on purpose, why would I have bothered to try and cover his light?" I reasoned.

The captain frowned, but did not immediately dismiss my argument. "And why would the tribesmen be after you?"

Leo sheathed his sword in a display of trust and nonaggression as he stepped closer to the captain. "For much the same reason they chase you, I imagine. We tend to prefer the rule of the old king—and the new."

Captain Jolene's eyes narrowed on Leo before widening when she looked at Orion. "You mean to tell me I am ferrying the lost prince on my ship?!"

"I am Sterling Astoria, son of Cedric and Hesperia Astoria, and Guildmaster of Hyperion." Orion gave a little bow. "I apologize for the secrecy and danger my presence brings."

"Prove it." Was it a trick of the light, or had her expression softened when she learned he was the Guildmaster?

"Excuse me?" Orion looked as startled as I felt. I could sense his panic as he tried to find a way out of admitting he could not grant wishes without the amulet's aid. I leaned into him, trying to convey my support, no matter what happened.

"Draw your starsteel blade and duel me." The pirate captain twirled her cutlass with practiced ease.

Orion hesitated, but then he drew his starsword. I was not the only one who gasped when the blade began to glow with a radiant silvery light. I glanced at Orion's face, and he seemed just as surprised as the rest of us. He had never held his sword while his hair was glowing like this before, but it made sense that the starsteel could channel and enhance the starlight he carried.

"No! Stop!" cried a young girl as she burst out of the cabin and raced to stand between Orion and the captain. A strange bird with dark, glittering feathers rode on her shoulder, one I had never seen before. "I will not let you hurt him!"

"Aria?" Orion cried in surprise, lowering his sword. Its glow illuminated the rough wooden planks beneath our feet. "What are *you* doing here?"

"Captain Jolene is the one who commissioned me to retrieve her starbird. When I brought it back, she offered me a place on her crew," the girl explained.

"Oh? And how do you know each other?" the captain drawled.

"Captain, this is the man I was telling you about, the one who helped me escape the tribesmen!" Aria exclaimed, gesturing to Orion. I raised an eyebrow. This was the first *I* was hearing of this.

"He is, is he?" She took a step closer, and I began to hope we might make it out of this bizarre situation unscathed. But my hopes were dashed when she raised her cutlass once more. "Then let us see what he is made of!"

A chorus of cheers went up from the surrounding crew, as they sheathed their weapons and formed a tight ring around us. I rested my hand on Orion's arm, silently asking if he wanted me to protest. Noctus and Leo watched for his response. But he simply shook his head, sending wisps of starlight into the air with the movement.

"Challenge accepted," he rumbled as he stepped forward into the ring of spectators. The others and I stepped back to join the ring as well, though Noctus looked none too happy about it.

The captain and Orion began to circle, each probing for an opening to attack. Jolene struck first, her cutlass lightning fast. But Orion blocked her flurry of blows, countering with a hail of his own. Orion seemed hesitant at first to go on the offensive against a woman, but the expert movements of his opponent soon convinced him otherwise.

Orion easily dodged a thrust at his chest, dancing to the side and swinging his glowing sword around towards the captain's shoulder. She brought up her guard just in time, and I tried not to wince at the screech of metal meeting metal. She snaked her blade around his in an attempt to fling it from his hands, sending sparks into the air to mix with the starlight of Orion's blade.

But Orion lunged forward, erasing her leverage so he could force her to disentangle her blade. Pressing his advantage, he chopped at her head, but I could tell he slowed enough so that the captain could easily duck. She scowled, realizing it too, and swept her cutlass at his legs to the cheers of her crew. Orion leaped into the air, using that momentum to bring his sword crashing down towards Jolene in a heavy arc.

The pirate threw herself to the side, rolling back to her feet in one fluid motion. A sudden gust of wind caused the deck to tilt as the ship rocked forward, and Orion stumbled. Before he could regain his balance, Jolene lunged forward with a smirk, the tip of her cutlass aimed at his chest.

My hand flew to my mouth and Noctus stiffened beside me, but a moment later Orion's sword flashed a blinding white, causing everyone to cover their eyes against its brilliance. I heard a clang and then a thud, and by the time my vision cleared, Orion was standing with the tip of his blade resting at the captain's neck. But the point of the crafty pirate's cutlass was snagged in the fabric over Orion's heart. Both were panting, but wore matching grins on their faces.

"A draw!" Leo announced, stepping forward.

There was a moment of silence from the crew, and I glanced around nervously. Would they take that as an affront to their captain and attack?

"That was amazing!" cried Aria as she bounded forward, the starbird letting out a cry, as if in agreement. "I want to learn how to sword fight too! Will you teach me?"

"You will have to learn to keep your balance on deck first. I saw the way you stumbled like the landlubbers at that little gust!" Captain Jolene laughed and sheathed her cutlass before ruffling the young teenager's hair.

Orion sheathed his blade as well, the glow fading from the metal once it was no longer in his hand. Noctus and I finally relaxed, and Rafe lowered his hackles. The crew began murmuring amongst themselves, but I was relieved to see none reached for their weapons.

"Good match," Orion said, holding his hand out to the captain.

"Likewise." She shook it heartily, her green eyes twinkling with mischief. "It seems I jumped to conclusions earlier. My apologies. If the newest member of our crew vouches for you, then I will take her at her word."

"I understand your caution. No harm was done." Orion accepted her apology gracefully.

Aria beamed at them both, her feathered friend ruffling its feathers and cocking its head at Orion. Suddenly, it hopped onto his shoulder, startling him, and began to run its beak through his still-glowing hair, as if it were preening him. It gave what I could only describe as a cry of delight, and when it opened its wings, small silver flecks in its feathers began to glow.

"Arcturus likes you, too!" Aria said with a laugh.

"He likes the starlight, not me," Orion grumbled. "The bird brain thinks I am his next meal." The starbird pecked him, as if it understood it was being insulted. "Ouch!"

Captain Jolene held out her hand, and after one final ruffle of Orion's hair, the bird hopped onto her shoulder. But it only stopped staring at Orion's hair when its glow finally faded.

"So, where are we taking our most unusual passengers?" she asked, her gaze sweeping over the rest of us as we came closer. The curse pulsed, stealing my breath for a few moments.

"To the Druidlands," Leo answered when I remained silent.

I fisted my hands in my tunic as I fought through the wave of pain the curse brought. It almost felt as if it had responded to the mere mention of the forest of its origination, but I knew that was nonsense.

"Not to Harland?" She glanced at Leo. "I had assumed he came as your guide."

"I am surprised you could tell," Leo said with a chuckle. "But then, like knows like. Nay, we seek allies a wee closer to home."

Captain Jolene grimaced. "I would say you might have better luck in Harland, but...the kingdom has seen better days."

Leo snorted. "It sounds like things have only gotten worse since I left."

"Unfortunately." Her eyes clouded for a moment before clearing again. "Well, I am happy to avoid returning to the Rocklands for as long as I can."

"You and me both," Leo agreed.

Captain Jolene turned to address her crew. "Set a course for the Druidlands!"

"Aye, aye, Captain!" replied a chorus of voices. At her order, the crew immediately set about trimming the sails and adjusting course in a flurry of activity.

"Allow me to show you to your room, um, Your Highness!" Aria offered eagerly. She was practically bouncing with excitement, and I hid my smile at the way she was fawning over Orion. I could hardly blame her for being a tad starstruck.

"Take the rest of the passengers to their cabins first. These two," she said, pointing at me and Orion, "will be coming with me."

Orion

I stayed close to Astrid as Jolene ushered us into what must have been the Captain's quarters. It was a neat and tidy cabin, with a comfortable bed in one corner and a writing desk in the other. Both were bolted into the floor, to prevent them from moving about during voyages. Maps of both sea and sky were tacked to the wooden walls and spread across the desk, with a large window above the desk providing an expansive view of the star-flecked sky.

I assumed the two smaller doors flanking the one we entered through led to her private privy and storage room. The only decorated item in the room was the large chest that sat at the foot of the bed, which had inlays of mother-of-pearl set to mimic the constellations.

"What else would you like to discuss?" I asked, standing awkwardly in the middle of the room.

The pirate did not answer immediately. She first securely fastened the door shut, pulled out the chair from beneath the desk, and gestured for Astrid and I to take a seat on her bed, which we reluctantly did. She sat down in the chair, facing us, with a stern expression on her features. I shifted uncomfortably, and Astrid touched her shoulder to mine in silent support.

But then, to my shock, she broke into a huge grin. "I cannot tell you how excited I am to meet you both! I can hardly believe that I have *the* Prince Sterling—who also happens to be Guildmaster Orion—and his right-hand healer on my ship! I have heard so much about you both!" She let out a girlish giggle that was very much at odds with her earlier gravitas.

My eyebrows shot towards my hairline, and I imagined Astrid wore a similar expression of surprise. Where had the tough pirate captain gone, and who was this starstruck, grinning lady?

"I am...flattered?" I said slowly, but my response seemed to satisfy her.

"Might I shake both of your hands?" Jolene practically squealed in excitement when I nodded, and rigorously shook both of our hands for far longer than seemed necessary.

Before either of us could figure out what to say, she continued, "I have been meaning to thank you both for some time now. You may not recall, but several years ago, you saved my young daughter, Charlotte, when she got tangled up in some rope in a terrible accident. She never told me how you did it, but she did share the bedtime story Astrid told her, about the mermaid and the star."

"I think I remember her," I murmured, a blurry memory surfacing of a dark-haired girl with vibrant green eyes and a ruined leg and arm. A point on my back warmed, likely the star that had signified her granted wish. "She did not cry, even though she must have been in a lot of pain, and she would tell anyone who would listen about her Captain Mama." I smiled at the memory. "How is she doing?"

The captain's eyes dimmed. "The plague took her, just before her birthday. She would have been fourteen this year."

"I am so sorry." Astrid reached out and took the woman's hands.

"By the time the symptoms showed, we were already halfway to Harland. Before we could even see Astoria on the horizon, she was already gone." Her eyes turned glassy, and my heart went out to her, even as my rage increased. Another innocent victim to lay at Nyra's feet.

"I wish we could have helped," I said thickly.

"Me too." The captain took a deep, shuddering breath. "But at least I now have the chance to repay you, for giving me at least a few more years with her."

"We very much appreciate your aid," Astrid said softly.

"Do you have business in the Druidlands as the Guildmaster or as the prince?" She cleared her throat, collecting herself, and patted Astrid's hands.

"As the prince," I replied. "I intend to form an alliance with the druids, since they are no doubt unhappy with the waves of tribesmen who have been passing through their forest to invade Astoria."

"They *are* quite touchy about trespassers," Jolene muttered with a scowl. "Still, I am surprised to hear you are not seeking aid from Harland. Does Astoria not have an amicable relationship with them?"

"More of a mutual disinterest. Astoria was originally founded by those fleeing the harshness of their laws, so their king is not overly friendly with us. If anything, I believe he saw us as a thorn in his side." At least, that had been my father's understanding. I shoved down the pang of grief that thought conjured. As if she could sense the direction of my thoughts, Astrid placed a hand on my knee, and I smiled gratefully at her.

"I see." Jolene's eyes flicked to Astrid's hand before returning to my face. "Perhaps Leo and I could be of assistance."

"How so?" Astrid asked.

"He served as a soldier, correct?"

"How could you tell?" I asked.

"The way he carries himself, and the scars he bears. Scars I bear as well." Jolene glanced down at her rough hands. "With his military connections, and my client relationships, we just might be able to arrange some key meetings."

"You believe Harland's king may be open to such an alliance?" I had dismissed the idea early on, since I did not think they would care to intervene in matters of the north, when their own people were already suffering from a poor economy and frequent witch attacks.

"I do." Jolene leveled her serious gaze at me. "If you offered enough starsteel to arm them against the witches and the tribesmen, they just might consider it."

I bowed my head, mulling it over. There was no stronger motivator than a mutual enemy to help one overlook past grievances. And I might not have to promise some outrageous wish that I was in no position to grant. Besides, if the druids rejected my proposal, it would be good to have another plan in place.

I raised my head. "I would like to commission you to ferry Leo to Harland with the aim of securing troops in exchange for starsteel."

Jolene grinned toothily. "Commission accepted."

"Now that that is settled, there is something I would like to ask," Astrid said into the silence.

"Ask away, my dear." The captain turned her attention to Astrid.

"If you decided to help us once you heard Orion's name, then why did you still insist on dueling him?"

That was a very good question—I had been wondering the same thing.

To my surprise, Jolene actually blushed, which looked odd on her normally stern and wind-chapped face. "In all honesty, I am not as tough as I portend to be. I still love dressing up, and teatime with my daughter was my favorite pastime." She smiled sadly.

"Then why put up a front?" Astrid asked with a smile.

"My crew really are tough as nails. I need to be even tougher to lead them." There was pride in her voice, and I could certainly understand the difficulty of having to lead a group of strong individuals.

"Well, you certainly had us fooled." I chuckled, thinking how wary I had been of her. Her two personas were very different from each other, but it somehow suited her.

"Glad to hear it. Now, I do believe I have something to discuss with my dear Astrid." She flapped her hands at me in a shooing motion.

Baffled, I slowly stood. What did those two have to discuss privately, after having only just met? I looked to Astrid, and she gave me a slight nod, so I dutifully made my way to the door. Although we had only known her a short while, I was surprised to realize that I trusted Jolene.

I grimaced as I made my way across the deck, dodging clingy members of the crew as I went. I had the sneaking suspicion that I would be participating in many more sparring matches before we reached Sylvaine, if the eager expressions on their faces were any indication. Like captain, like crew.

Astrid

"Why did you send Orion out?" I asked, confused. What would the pirate and I have to talk about?

"There is something I wanted to confirm with you." She took Orion's place beside me on the bed, and I watched her warily.

She lifted a lock of my hair, her emerald eyes examining the blackened ends that slowly lightened to the mousy brown I had known all my life. She rubbed the burnt-looking strands between her fingers, and I bit my lip, nervous.

"What happened here?" Her eyes finally lifted from my hair.

"Dying the tips of one's hair is in fashion in Astoria these days." I tugged my hair from her grasp, concealing a wince when a few of the brittle strands broke off and floated to the ground. It seemed to grow weaker every day.

"Is that so?" I could tell from her tone that she did not believe me.

"Yes, though I have found the two different shades distracting, so I plan on dying the rest to match in the near future," I lied with a weak smile, before rising from the bed. "If that is all, I will take my leave and join the others."

Jolene rose as well, quick as a striking snake, and grabbed my arm. She pushed back the sleeves of my tunic, baring the darkened veins that wrapped around my wrists.

"Why are you hiding it?" Her eyes pierced into mine, searching for something, but I looked away.

Just then, I felt the now-familiar stab in my core that always preceded the effects of the curse. I stumbled as a gut-wrenching pain stole my vision, turning the world white, and my ears rang as I gasped for breath. I felt strong arms catch me as I fell, and it was all I could do to try not to faint. Every shallow breath sent a stabbing pain through my heart, forcing me to focus only on drawing what little breath I could.

I clenched my sightless eyes shut as I thrashed, my muscles trying to fight the source of the pain. But it was emanating from the wellspring of my unsealed magic, where no remedy could reach. I could feel the disgustingly slimy touch of the corruption as it consumed my magic, weakening me to strengthen itself like some sort of magical parasite.

I tried to clear my mind, to think of anything but the waves of pain and panic rolling through me. This was the worst attack so far, and the first to occur when I was not alone. I would have to be more attentive to the warning signs, to make sure I did not derail Orion's attempts to save his kingdom, his people. I pictured his smiling face, his glowing hair like a halo around his head, the miniature stars that created a crown more regal than any king's. I pictured the excited faces of Nova and Castor when I taught them a new remedy, the pride on Sirius' face when Estelle read to him aloud for the first time.

I reminded myself that we were doing this for them, for every member of the family we had chosen.

After a few minutes of this absolute agony, my frenzied magic finally calmed, weakened into slumber. I was able to slowly take deep breaths as the pain receded, and the wooden ceiling swam into view above me. My senses cleared, and I realized that Jolene was holding me against her, murmuring soothing words and stroking my damp forehead.

"There you are, dear. It is all right. You are safe," Jolene murmured.

I blinked slowly as the room came into focus.

"How did you know?" I rasped weakly, even as my cheeks flamed in humiliation and sorrow. No one had held me like this since I had lost my mother to the same curse.

"A little less than two decades ago, before I was blessed with a daughter of my own, I gave passage to a druid mother and her infant. She was fleeing the Druidlands, and no other captain would allow her to board their vessels, not when her beautiful blonde hair was blackening and her veins and eyes were darkening. They believed she had been hexed by a witch, and refused to risk the lives of themselves or their crew." My eyes slowly widened as she spoke, disbelief slowly giving way to understanding.

"You knew my mother." My eyes found hers, and she nodded sadly.

"Aye. Though I was reluctant at first, I eventually agreed to give her passage aboard this very ship after I heard her tale. It took a night of ale and begging to convince the rest of the crew, though." She chuckled drily at the memory.

"What did she tell you?" I was desperate to learn anything I could about my mother, about the tragedy that had chased her to Astoria like a phantom in the night.

"She told a beautiful and heartbreaking tale, the kind I had only encountered in tragic plays." Jolene ran a hand over my hair as she gathered her thoughts, her unfocused eyes gazing towards the star-filled windows.

"As an adept wielder of wild magic, your mother fought many battles against the witches, who would descend upon their lush forest from the rocky mountains like a cloud of locusts. Weary from a long day of fighting, your mother was unable to deflect a witch's hex of poison, which took root in her shoulder and began to spread. Thinking the poison would finish her off, the witch left her to die a slow and painful death at the edge of the forested border with Harland."

"Was that how...?" I trailed off. My mother had never told me the tale of how she met my father.

"Yes. A soldier stumbled across her, and was instantly struck by the dying druid's beauty. By law, he was bound to report her to his commander, so that she might be conscripted into the army, to fight for his king. But he had seen the dull eyes of a captured druid before, and the horrid conditions and treatment he endured, and refused to condemn your mother to the same fate. Instead, he brought her back to his dwelling to tend to her wounds. At great risk to himself, he stole a pinch of rare stardust, the only thing that could have cured your mother of the witch's hex. Her recovery was slow, but the human shared what little he had, and the two soon fell in love.

"For years, she stayed with him, hiding her pointed ears with hats and dying her blonde hair a common brown. She knew that those she had left behind believed her to be either dead or captured, but she feared the wrath and disapproval of her kin for her forbidden relationship with a human. Despite the spectre of discovery hanging over them, she described those years as the happiest of her life." A small smile graced Jolene's chapped lips, and I eagerly soaked up every word.

"The druids found out, though," I murmured sadly, wishing for a happy ending I knew I would never hear.

Jolene sighed. "When she realized she was with child, her fear only grew. She rarely ventured outside, and used her connection with nature to have animals scare off any humans or druids who came too close. Alas, that would be her undoing.

"Not long after she brought her darling daughter into the world, the druids investigated the strange behavior of the animals, fearing some new witch's scheme. At first, her kin were overjoyed to discover her alive and well, when they had believed her lost. But when her father and the elders discovered what she had done, they became enraged, and demanded that she destroy her child to atone, and to maintain the purity of their blood and their magic."

Horror washed over me. "She was condemned simply for loving a human, and having a child with him?" What kind of *monsters* were these druids?

Jolene nodded sadly. "When she refused, her father came after her, determined to destroy you if she would not. Your father tried valiantly to protect you, and even managed to strike a devastating blow against your grandfather. But your father was gravely wounded, and in his rage and pain, your grandfather cast a horrible curse upon you and your mother. It was a forbidden technique, a corruption of the pure wild magic of the druids. It would eat away at the magic and lifeforce of the afflicted, consuming them from the inside out."

"That is what killed my mother. And what is going to kill me." I raised my wrist, my darkening veins even more pronounced in the flickering candlelight. Jolene put her hand over mine, hiding the corruption from sight.

"She was captured and taken back to the forest, where she was confined in a cell. Since her father had fallen unconscious from his injury, the druids were waiting to conduct an investigation and trial. But before he awoke, a sympathetic druid helped smuggle you and your mother out of the forest, which is when she made her way to our dock."

"So *one* druid is not a monster." I scoffed, my eyes misting at the thought of what my mother had gone through because of me. No, because of her nightmarish father. She had never told me—perhaps to protect me, or because I was too young to understand.

"She planned to beg for her wish to be granted in Astoria, to save you from sharing her fate. Her heartbreak was so great that without you, she may have been content to remain in her cell." Jolene rubbed calming circles on the back of my hand. "I had assumed she succeeded, when I saw you standing beside Orion. How is it that you and the curse are coexisting? And why have you not even told the prince, let alone asked him to save you?"

My gaze found the distant stars through her window, and I swallowed painfully. "My mother met with Queen Hesperia just after she had given birth to her son. She begged her to save me from the curse, but weakened as she was from childbirth, it took everything she had just to seal my magic, and the curse along with it."

I heard Jolene's sharp intake of breath as she put the pieces together, and I slowly turned my tortured gaze on her heartbroken face. "I only recently learned that my guildmaster was actually the prince. After he saved me from slavers and gave my life purpose, how could I possibly ask him for the same thing that cost him his mother?"

"It was not your fault, little star," Jolene whispered as her own eyes misted.

"*I* am the reason he lost his mother! And I cannot bear to tell him!" I sat up, only for Jolene to pull me into a hug as the tears came, flowing unchecked down my cheeks. "And now that that evil woman has killed his father and stolen his amulet, he can no longer grant wishes. How could I tell him *now?!* He would only worry about me, and that would distract him from retaking Astoria. I *refuse* to be the reason the kingdom of the stars falls, not when I have already taken its queen!"

Jolene rubbed my back soothingly as I sobbed, my pent-up fear and frustration pouring from me like a burst dam. It was hard to stay strong when she looked at me with those kind and motherly eyes.

"I do not know of this amulet, but it seemed to me he does have some magic in him, what with that glowing hair of his," Jolene eventually murmured as the worst of my sobs subsided.

"I think he did not know he had inherited any of his mother's magic until just recently—he and the king had been using a magical amulet his mother made to grant wishes all this time. I saw him grant a wish without it once, to save a friend's life. But that was almost an accident—I do not think he truly knows how to use his magic, and there is no one left to teach him," I said haltingly.

"If she sealed your magic and the curse, why has it resurfaced?" she asked quietly.

I sniffled. "Nyra nearly killed him, right after she killed his father. I broke the seal to save him from her blade, and again to cure him of her poison."

"You love him." It was more of a statement than a question.

"W-What?!" I exclaimed, startled. I leaned back, away from Jolene.

"I can hear it in your voice." She sounded amused, but there was no judgment in her sea-green eyes.

I blushed, looking down. "Is it so obvious?"

"To me, perhaps." She chuckled. "That boy has no clue, though, does he?"

I shook my head, laughing shakily. "Not even the faintest."

"You should tell him." Jolene gripped my shoulders gently.

"Did you not listen to a word I said? What point is there in telling him when I have so little time left?" I scowled. "I want our remaining moments to be happy ones."

"He deserves to know, both how you feel and about this curse." Her eyes were serious, but not unkind. "What he decides to do after is up to him. But at least he will have that choice. Please, do not take that from him."

"But I am afraid," I whispered hoarsely, my stomach tightening at the thought of baring my soul to him.

"More afraid than when you agreed to return with him to the place your mother fled?" Jolene arched one bushy eyebrow.

"Yes." I gave her a watery smile.

"If you were brave enough to save him, knowing you were dooming yourself, I think you are brave enough to tell him the truth." She pulled me back into her embrace, and I closed my eyes, knowing she was right. "And I will do everything I can to help you in the meantime. Starting with loading you down with as much starsteel and stardust as I can find to slow down that curse."

Orion

The next day, I yawned and wiped the sleep from my eyes as I emerged onto the deck. I had grown far too accustomed to the quiet solitude of my rooms in the castle; I had hardly slept a wink all night, thanks to the irregular rocking motion of the ship. And just as I had finally begun to drift off, the crew's flurry of activity around dawn ensured I was wide awake. So I had decided to see if I could make myself useful.

I nodded to Noctus when I spotted him lurking in one of the only spots of shadow on deck. It seemed I was not the only one who had not slept.

The clang of steel against steel met my ears in bursts, as the winds either snatched the sound away or carried it to me. Silhouetted against the sunrise, Captain Jolene and Leo were enthusiastically sparring. Several of the crew watched with keen interest, though several were only sneaking glances while feigning busyness with some nearby task or other.

I walked over to them on still-unsteady legs, though I was careful to leave the combatants plenty of room. I leaned against the foremast to watch, and was impressed with what I saw.

The captain easily parried Leo's thrust, only to counter with a strike of her own. Leo grunted as his sword arm took the brunt of the forceful blow, causing Jolene to laugh.

"A little rusty, old man?" she called in between strikes.

"As rusty as your tongue!" he barked back, but I could see the way the corner of his mouth curved upwards beneath his beard.

"Keep up then, would you?" Her eyes lit up at the challenge he presented.

"Oh, but I have yet to warm up!"

If I did not know any better, I would have assumed they were flirting. And I could guess who had initiated, based on how much fun Jolene seemed to be having.

He lunged forward and she dodged, nimble as a rabbit. Leo stumbled when the deck tilted in a sudden gust, and Jolene took advantage of that moment to whack him across the rear with the flat of her blade. I stifled a laugh, the crew members nearby not even bothering to conceal their grins.

"Oho, is that how it is going to be?" Leo roared in mock indignation.

He went charging at the pirate like a bull in a china shop, delivering a ruthless series of blows that rained down on the captain's firm defenses.

"It will be until you get your flying legs under you!" Jolene laughed, looking none too bothered by the fact that she was slowly being forced back.

"I will show you flying legs!"

Without warning, Leo kicked out a leg, which he hooked behind Jolene's knees. Before she knew what was happening, Leo had swept her legs out from under her, and she landed square on her back. I heard the breath leave her lungs in a great *whoosh,* and before she could move to defend herself, Leo had positioned the tip of his blade to one side of her head, and planted his hand on the other. She was trapped, though I saw her begin to raise the tip of her cutlass towards Leo's exposed back before she let it fall back to the deck.

"That was cheating, old man," Jolene said with a chuckle once she could breathe again. "But I will yield for today."

I heard a few gasps of surprise from the nearby crew members, and surmised that either watching their captain be bested or hearing her admit defeat was a rarity. I noticed they began eyeing Leo with renewed interest, and I smiled at the thought that Leo was about to have a hoard of new challengers.

"All is fair in love and war," Leo retorted, though his tongue tripped on the word love, as if he had surprised even himself.

"It appears I am interrupting...something," I said as I pushed off the foremast and walked over to them, waggling my eyebrows suggestively.

Leo seemed to suddenly realize that he was still pinning Jolene to the deck in a rather compromising position. The grizzled soldier actually blushed as he hastily scrambled to his feet, and could hardly look the pirate in the eye as he offered her a hand up.

She took it, letting him pull her to her feet. She was grinning like a cat with a fish, and I was incredibly amused until she turned that gaze on me.

"Your turn next, princeling."

I blinked. "Excuse me? Was last night's match not enough to prove myself to you?"

"Oh, that was plenty. But an idle blade goes rusty, and yours will need to be as keen as broken glass for where you are headed, my boy." Suddenly I felt much more sympathy for Leo.

"You make a compelling point," I replied reluctantly. I began to stretch out my arms and legs to warm them up after a cramped night below decks.

Leo clapped me on the back. "Good luck, son. You are going to need it."

"Thanks for that vote of confidence," I grumbled, but dutifully drew my sword as Leo drew back to join the spectators.

I raised the tip of my sword and began to circle Jolene, watching her warily. Last night's win had been a stroke of luck; she and I both knew it. But the shape of her sword was more similar to Nyra's than those of any other opponent I had fought, so I knew this would be good practice for the day I held Nyra to account for what she has done.

Seeing an opening, I darted forward, delivering some probing strikes. She blocked them easily enough, and managed to counterattack a handful of times. But then she took me by surprise when she feinted to one side, only to roll to the other side and swipe at my legs. I jumped back, and while I tried to regain my balance, she lunged in close. Our blades met in a clash of steel, and this time I was the one on the defensive.

"Why all the tricks?" I grunted as I continued to parry.

"Your moves are far too uniform and entirely predictable, princeling." She forced me back another step. "If you are going to defeat anyone other than a knight, you will need to learn how to fight like a pirate."

She grinned at me, and I realized sheepishly that I had, in fact, been fighting as if I were sparring with Sir Rigel or one of the other knights. I gritted my teeth, attempting to recall some of the sessions with Sirius, whose strategies were based on street fights and tavern brawls.

Changing tactics, I hid one foot behind the other, turning my body like an opening door, and allowed Jolene's momentum to carry her past me. I grinned at the surprised look on her face and slashed my sword at her exposed back.

She hit the deck and rolled, popping back up like a swordswoman half her age. But I refused to let up, throwing more feints into my patterns and forcing her to turn so that the rising sun shone directly into her eyes. When she squinted against the glare, I dropped down low to sweep her legs out from under her, but she somehow managed to hop to the side.

"Nice try, but that trick will not work on me twice." She chuckled as we began to circle once more.

Sweat dripped from my brow, and both of our breathing was becoming labored. Jolene slowly brought her blade up, holding it parallel to the deck. I frowned, but realized the trick too late. She tilted the blade so that the sun bounced right into my eyes, causing me to squint.

All it took were those precious few moments of distraction for her to lunge forward and level her cutlass at my neck, in an eerily similar pose to the one Nyra had taken, when she had me on my knees before her, poisoned and delirious. A twisted sense of rage and fear roiled in my stomach at the visceral reminder of my near-death experience. My knuckles turned white as I squeezed the hilt of my starsword, and I peeled my lips back in a grin that felt more like a snarl.

Jolene was right. I never wanted to be at another's mercy like this again.

"Better. I think you have an idea now of where you can improve," Jolene commented approvingly as she withdrew her cutlass, sheathing it at her hip once more. "I like that look in your eye."

"Another round?" I asked, trying to slow my breathing.

"Wait your turn, boy. Noctus and I would also like a go," Leo said good-naturedly as he and Noctus joined us.

"Come, I will fight both of you at once!" The pirate put both hands on her hips, and I was impressed by her spirit.

I stepped back to lean against the foremast once more, content to watch how Jolene handled fighting more than one opponent. As the trio began dancing around each other, I noted how the captain used their lack of teamwork against them. She also had this nasty habit of using whatever underhanded tactic she could think up to get the upper hand.

My father and Sir Magnus would have surely disapproved of such less-than-honorable combat. But perhaps if they had set aside their pride, they would have both still been here. My lips twisted in a bittersweet smile. There was no point in thinking such things now, except to learn from their mistakes.

Astrid, Adelaide and Rafe finally joined us on deck, and paused to watch as Jolene sparred with Leo and Noctus. Both were generally holding their own, though I noticed Noctus refrained from using his throwing knives. After all, with the sudden gusts of wind on a tilting deck, he was just as likely to miss or lose them over the side of the ship as he was to actually hit anything. Jolene definitely had the terrain advantage here.

As the sun climbed above the horizon and then began its ascent, Aria appeared as well, the starbird riding on her thin shoulder. She went straight to Astrid, and after a short discussion, the pair began to set up a barrel lid as a make-shift target to shoot arrows at, while Adelaide and Rafe continued to watch the sparring from a safe distance.

Aria was clearly a novice, but Astrid seemed to enjoy giving her some pointers. But her face still seemed rather drawn. I had no idea what Astrid had discussed with Jolene last night, but it was clearly still affecting her. Her eyes were a little puffy, and my stomach lurched when I realized that meant she had been crying.

That reminded me of when that tribesman had hurt her, and set my blood boiling. I pushed off the foremast, intending to go and ask what was bothering her, when Jolene called me over.

"Your turn, princeling!"

I looked over to see Leo flat on his back and Noctus bent over with his hands on his knees, panting quietly. After another glance at Astrid, I made my way over.

I unsheathed my sword and jumped into the sparring match with renewed vigor. I had a lot to learn from this pirate, and wanted to make the most of every moment. By starship, the journey between the heart of Astoria and the border with the Druidlands should only take about two weeks, barring any storms. I intended to spar with her, Leo, and Noctus as many times as they would allow within that time.

Despite my intentions, however, I could not help but glance at Astrid whenever she and Aria came into view. Astrid was smiling down at Aria as she corrected the way she held her small bow, but it was still not as bright as usual. Would she be willing to confide in me? Or would bringing it up only chase away her smile completely?

Jolene's cutlass crashed into mine, sending a jarring pain up my arm, and bringing my attention back to our match.

"Should you really allow yourself to be distracted like this?" Jolene said with a wicked gleam in her eye.

"What did you discuss with her last night that made her so upset?" I asked before I could think better of it. I shoved her backwards but she came right back to lock blades with me again.

"That is something you should ask *her*—though I am disappointed you have yet to notice on your own," she grunted.

"She has a bad habit of keeping her problems to herself," I ground out, a tad defensively.

"Sounds like someone else I know," Jolene taunted, raising an eyebrow at me.

I risked another glance at Astrid, and was surprised to see that she was looking at me. Our gazes locked for an instant before I had to defend against the pirate's next strike. Had I spoken too loudly? Had Astrid overheard? Did I want her to?

We locked blades once more, allowing me to experiment with how to better deal with a curved blade. My straight sword limited my options in a way that hers did not. But I forgot all about that when Jolene next spoke.

"So, princeling, how long have you been courting Astrid?"

Astrid

S hooting at some make-shift targets with Aria while Jolene and the boys sparred helped to take my mind off of things. Though simply having someone to share my secrets with had done wonders for me. Just as Jolene suggested, I had consumed some stardust this morning, and I could feel it suppressing both my own magic and the corrupted curse that fed off of it. I had not felt so light and comfortable in weeks.

I should have been more grateful for every pain-free day I had the pleasure of experiencing when my magic was still sealed. I had taken breathing easily for granted, so I savored the sensation now.

I could not help glancing between Adelaide and Orion, though. At first I assumed Adelaide had simply been watching the sparring for lack of anything better to do; but now it looked as if it were Orion she was watching, and not the matches. I felt a whisper of unease at that observation, but I tried to reason it away as my overactive emotions from last night lingering.

"I did it! I hit the target this time!" Aria pumped her fist in the air, and the starbird rustled its feathers in annoyance at the motion.

I almost reluctantly returned my gaze to the wooden barrel lid we had propped up against the mainmast. "Well done, Aria!"

"Now it is your turn, Astrid!" The younger girl watched me expectantly, and I smiled down at her as I nocked an arrow to the bowstring and pulled it back to my ear.

I took an extra moment to aim, to account for the gusty winds that swirled across the deck, before letting the arrow fly. The sharp arrowhead buried itself in the wood, just a hair off from center. I must have overcompensated for the wind, then. But Aria was just as excited as if I had hit dead-center.

"If I keep practicing, can I do that too?" Aria asked as she came back from retrieving our two arrows, and handed me mine.

"Absolutely." I ruffled her hair, pulling my fingers back just in time to avoid a peck from the bird. "The trick is in correcting your aim to account for the wind. Keep at it, and I know you will get the hang of it in no time."

I slung my bow over my back as I turned to walk over to Adelaide and Rafe. As I did, I glanced over at Orion again, and wondered if this was sparring match number five or seven this morning. His dark hair was damp with sweat, his tunic was plastered to his well-defined chest, and I noticed he wore some sort of necklace under his tunic, with a pendant that looked vaguely star-shaped. Had he started wearing a substitute for the amulet to fill the void it had left behind?

I was more than a little surprised when his eyes met mine, and I felt a hint of warmth rise in my cheeks. But I quickly looked away, telling myself not to read into it. He was likely just curious about what Jolene and I had discussed last night.

"Adelaide, would you help me with something belowdecks?" I gave Rafe a few idle pets, and his tail wagged in response.

"Whatever you need." She smiled, but was it just me, or did she seem reluctant to tear her eyes away from Orion?

I led the way down into the shadowy depths of the hull to my cabin, Adelaide's boots echoing on the wood behind me, accompanied by the clicking of Rafe's claws. I grabbed my satchel and brought it over to the desk that was bolted into the wall and the floor, withdrawing a few key ingredients.

Adelaide frowned as she scanned the various herbs and berries. "None of your recipes call for these ingredients."

"Adelaide, I was hoping you would help me create an antidote that can counter the hypnotic effects of the desert's sandberries. I have a feeling that Orion is going to need protection from them. Everyone in the kingdom might, in fact."

Her dark eyes lit up with excitement. "You mean to create a brand-new antidote? With my help?"

"Yes! I could really use your expertise on this," I said with a smile as I pulled out two chairs. "What do you say?"

"Absolutely! I mean," Adelaide cleared her throat, trying to tone down her excitement. "If you need my help so badly, I would not mind assisting you."

Rafe glanced up at the excited look on her face, curled up in a sunny spot on the floor, and heaved a great sigh as he laid his head on his paws, almost as if he knew Adelaide would not be moving from this spot for quite some time.

"Why did Jolene call a meeting?" I asked Orion quietly as I joined him on deck.

Adelaide and Rafe emerged behind me, squinting in the brightness of the sunset. We had become so absorbed in our work that the whole day had passed before we knew it. And based on the rather exhausted faces of Orion, Noctus, and Leo, they had been sparring for the better part of the day.

"Not sure." He shook his head.

I bit my lip, and fiddled idly with the tip of my brittle braid before the texture began to bother me. I had not exacted a vow of silence from Jolene after our conversation last night, but surely she was not about to reveal what I had told her in confidence to everyone here, right? I glanced around nervously as most of the crew assembled as well.

"Did she say anything...unusual?" I pressed. He slipped his hand into mine, surprising me and sending a little thrill through me.

"Well, she did ask some odd questions about Adelaide and Rafe during our last match." He frowned. "But I see no reason why that should warrant a meeting."

Once everyone was assembled, Jolene stepped into the center of our loose circle and looked around at everyone. Some unspoken signal passed between the crew, and their expressions smoothed into blank masks.

"It has come to my attention that one of our guests has been keeping a serious secret, and I felt it was my duty to inform the others, before that secret puts their whole mission in jeopardy. Originally, I assumed everyone knew, but it would appear that is not the case."

Orion stiffened beside me, and my stomach twisted. I caught Jolene's eye, but the slight shake of her head did not tell me much.

Suddenly, Jolene whirled, drawing her cutlass and pointing it at Adelaide. "Witches are not welcome on the *StarSeeker*."

Before anyone could react, two of the crew had restrained her arms behind her back, and pressed a starsteel dagger to her throat. Adelaide's expression was one of fear and shock, and I saw her dark eyes flicker, turning a shocking red. No, it was the illusion she had cast that had faded on contact with starsteel. This must be her natural eye color, the one I had briefly glimpsed when we first met. I had guessed at her secret, and had hoped to hear it from her lips once the trust between us was greater.

"A witch?! We should not have trusted her," Orion ground out, the pain of Nyra's betrayal no doubt surfacing in his mind.

Rafe snapped at the two crewmembers, growling deep in his chest, his hackles raised menacingly. Orion pulled me behind him protectively and drew his sword, Noctus and Leo following suit.

"Her familiar," muttered a few of the crew, curling their lips at the wolf.

"I was going to tell them," Adelaide protested.

"When? Once the druids had accused them of bringing an enemy spy into their forest?" Jolene scoffed, advancing.

"Of course not!" Adelaide retorted, but then her tone softened. "I was going to tell them before we arrived. I just...I had yet to work up the courage, because I feared their reactions would be..." she trailed off, then laughed bitterly. "Well, that they would be afraid of me, just like this."

"That still does not explain what a witch is doing in Astoria." Orion finally stepped forward, watching Adelaide warily. He kept me close behind him. "Are you some sort of spy, sent by Nyra? What did she promise you as payment?"

"I am no one's spy!" Adelaide spat, her eyes hard and angry. "I was cast out of my own coven, after enduring their abuse my entire life! And Rafe is not my familiar—I rescued him from his fate of becoming a sacrifice."

"And you expect me to believe that?" Orion scoffed.

"She does bear many scars," I murmured quietly, remembering the thin lines I had seen on the skin of her hands and arms that had not been covered by her dark clothes.

Adelaide went silent for a moment. "Why do you think I look nothing like the other witches?"

Orion faltered. I was fairly certain he had seen witches before, in his capacity as prince. "Witches can transform their appearances with hexes."

"Not while starsteel touches our skin," she pointed out, glancing meaningfully at the metal blade pressed to her throat. "The only thing I hid was the color of my eyes."

"Why, then?" Orion asked guardedly.

"My magic was sealed until recently, with corrupted starsteel. I have never harmed a human, nor do I plan to." Her declaration momentarily shocked all of us. Was it even possible to corrupt starsteel?

"Starsteel cannot be corrupted." There was a trace of uncertainty in Orion's voice now.

"See for yourself. The necklace welded around my throat was corrupted with a powerful hex, and is dampening the majority of my magic even now." Adelaide puffed out her chest, and after a nod from Jolene, one of the crew stepped forward to reveal the choker necklace that had been hidden beneath her scarf.

I gasped at the angry red welts that surrounded the collar-like necklace. One large star with two smaller stars sat on the front, and unlike the starsteel I was familiar with, this one was tarnished. I could sense a flicker of malevolent magic from it, a sensation not wholly different from the curse that dwelled within me. How had I missed it?

My heart went out to her. We were kindred spirits, she, and I. Both cursed and cast out of our homelands, by the very people who were meant to protect us.

I slipped my hand out of Orion's and went up to Adelaide, reaching out a hand that stopped just short of touching the tarnished metal. I raised my eyes to hers, the fear in them striking a familiar chord.

But Orion narrowed his eyes. "That does not change the fact that you deceived us, and very nearly cost me my audience with the druids. Since you have been with us for some time now, you know that the fate of my kingdom depends on this."

After a moment, Adelaide slowly lowered her red eyes. "I am sorry."

"Why did you continue to hide it from us?" I asked softly. I felt like a hypocrite asking that question, but I knew it was something we needed to hear.

"Because..." When Adelaide hesitated, Rafe whined, as if encouraging her to be honest. "Because I did not want to be cast out again."

For a moment, only the sound of the wind could be heard on deck, as everyone digested what Adelaide had said.

"Yours is not the only sob story here, and I prefer not to take my chances. I have half a mind to throw you and your wolf off my ship this instant," Jolene announced. Rafe stepped in between them, growling menacingly.

"I think we should give her a second chance." Adelaide's eyes met mine, flying wide in surprise. "She has been a great help to us so far, and by her actions alone she has done no wrong."

"Though I certainly do not condone her deceit, I can understand why she did what she did," Leo finally spoke, stepping up beside me. I smiled up at him, and he winked at me.

"This comes as a surprise," Jolene said, her eyes flicking between Leo and I, before she turned to Orion. "Well, princeling? What shall we do with the witch?"

Orion's gaze locked with mine, and I silently pleaded with him to spare her life.

"Orion, please. I will take responsibility for her," I added for good measure.

The tense moment stretched out, but Orion's eyes never left mine. Eventually, he said, "She can stay—only because it is Astrid who is asking. I trust her judgment more than mine on this. But the alliance with the druids remains my priority. Should she put its completion in jeopardy..." He let the unspoken warning hang in the air, but Adelaide nodded in calm acceptance.

Warmth bloomed in my chest at Orion's trust in me, and I breathed a sigh of relief as Jolene reluctantly nodded at her girls. The starsteel dagger was withdrawn from Adelaide's neck and she was released. Rafe gave my hand a lick before he took up his place beside his witch.

"How do we know you have not cast a hex upon any of us?" Noctus said into the stiff silence, and I saw several of the crew nod.

Adelaide glanced at me and then at Orion. "He would have felt the use of magic that strong. The only reason he did not sense the glamour on my eyes seems to be because he has little practice using his own magic."

My stomach twisted. Had she glanced at me because she could sense my magic, corrupted though it may be? Had she known this whole time?

"*My* magic?" Orion echoed, frowning. "No, you must be sensing the residual magic in my pendant."

I looked over at him, confused by the fact that he would openly mention the amulet, and that he was implying that the one he currently wore also held magic. But then his words fully hit me, and my jaw nearly dropped in surprise. But before I could say anything, Adelaide beat me to it.

Adelaide rubbed at her arms where the crew had held her. "Wait, do you mean to tell me..." Her lips parted in shock. "Do you mean to tell me that you are unaware that you have the power of a fallen star?"

Astrid

"Are... Are you sure?" Orion stammered, his blue eyes wide with confusion and a little bit of hope. Jolene and the crew listened with rapt attention.

"Absolutely. Magic knows magic." There was no doubt in Adelaide's voice, and that seemed to reassure him.

"I had no idea. I assumed the magic came only from the amulet." Orion frowned, looking down.

"There *is* some magic in the pendant you wear now, but it is a mere spark in comparison to the magic that is in you." Adelaide cocked her head, her unsettling red eyes scanning Orion from head to toe. "That must be why your magic spills out and changes your appearance when you touch starlight, or when your emotions get away from you—you have yet to learn to wield it properly."

Orion nodded slowly, as if thinking back on every time his hair had glowed silver in the past month. "That would explain much. But why did my appearance never change when I used my amulet before?"

"I think before, you were simply channeling the amulet's power, as your father did," I said quietly. "The night everything changed was when you granted a wish without using the amulet."

Orion's eyes widened. "I had meant to use my own lifeforce to power the wish and save Rigel, but I think I unconsciously tapped into my own...magic instead." He held his hands up before him, turning them over in wonder as if he had never seen them before.

I nodded. "It was only after that night that you began glowing at night." So my guess had been right; the cost of granting a wish without enough magic to power it was steep indeed. I was incredibly grateful Orion had not had to trade his life for Rigel's.

I felt a tiny glimmer of hope at the thought that if he had saved Rigel without sacrificing any of his own lifeforce, that he could do the same to save mine. But I quickly squashed that hope before it could blossom. There was a huge difference between healing a wound and undoing a powerful magical curse. The risk was too great.

Orion went quiet, contemplating this new revelation. Everything had happened so quickly, and then after losing his father and nearly losing his own life...it was no wonder Orion had not realized the meaning of it all. I think I had assumed that his abilities were thanks to his parentage, but I was still surprised to discover that he himself had had no clue. I should have said something.

"I would offer to teach you, but I am afraid only another fallen star could properly instruct you." Adelaide tentatively broke the silence.

"The offer is appreciated," Orion smiled genuinely at Adelaide for the first time since Jolene had revealed her secret.

"You now have much greater bargaining power, my friend," Leo said as he clapped Orion on the back.

"And an even greater target on your back," Jolene muttered, glancing worriedly at me, but Orion's grin did not dim.

He glanced at me, and I could see how relieved he felt to know that he had the capacity to grant wishes. I, on the other hand, felt almost...disappointed. If I were being honest with myself, it had almost been a relief to think that Orion could never share the same fate as his mother. But now...now that unthinkable option was there once more, hovering like a phantom over our heads. I shivered involuntarily, and tried to put it out of my mind.

"Well, if we are not throwing anybody overboard, then I say we break for supper," Jolene announced as she sheathed her cutlass.

Adelaide looked relieved, and I smiled at her reassuringly. Noctus whispered something to Orion, and I saw him frown, then nod after a moment. I noticed that many of the crew gave

Adelaide a wide berth and cast dark looks her way, but she seemed largely unbothered by their reactions. Even Aria was suddenly nervous around her, and kept at a safe distance.

As a display of trust, I went over to Adelaide and Rafe, and walked with them to join the others for a supper of warm stew.

That night, I lay awake in my hammock, my mind too full of thoughts and my body too full of pain to allow me to drift off to sleep. I stared blindly into the darkness, replaying the earlier confrontation over and over again. Guilt nipped at me, and I wondered for the hundredth time since this afternoon if I should also come clean to Orion. But what if he then decided to leave me behind, or send me away while he continued on alone to the Druidlands?

I did not want to spend what little time I had left alone. I wanted to stay by his side for as long as I could. Was that too selfish of me?

The gentle rocking motion of the ship did little to soothe me. I curled up in a ball as another wave of pain stole my breath, trying to ride the wave out. There was a near-constant ache in my core now, in the center of my being where my magic lived. I screwed my eyes shut and focused on breathing until the wave of pain subsided.

Doubting I would be getting any sleep after that, I climbed out of my hammock and slipped on my boots, fumbling a bit in the darkness. I padded through the hull of the ship and scaled the ladder onto the deck. The wind cooled my clammy skin, a welcome change from the humid rooms below. I glanced around, noting that only a few members of the crew were present, to make sure the ship did not veer off course during the night.

But then my gaze snagged on a lone male figure leaning against the railing and gazing up at the expansive field of stars above us. He was easy to spot thanks to the way his hair glowed with silvery starlight.

I made my way over to him, my dilemma from earlier pushing back to the forefront of my mind. Should I tell him?

My steps faltered when I saw him swipe at his eyes, and realized he must be missing his parents tonight. Being so much closer to the stars, while still being too far to reach them, must have felt like a special kind of torment.

"Trouble sleeping?" I asked as I joined him at the railing.

He nodded. "You too?"

"Yes."

We both gazed up at the stars in comfortable silence for a time, each lost in our own thoughts. The stars were certainly beautiful, and looked nearly close enough to touch. I wondered if Queen Hesperia was one of the stars looking down on us right now. I hoped she had seen how I had saved her son, and hoped that would bring her some solace, knowing her sacrifice had saved her own son as well.

Movement caught my eye, and I squinted up at a peculiar patch of darkness that almost seemed to be...moving. I heard Orion's deep chuckle beside me, and turned to see him watching me.

"What?" I asked defensively, feeling my cheeks grow warm.

"It can be hard to make out, but that odd shape up there is the captain's starbird. The reason they are so hard to capture is because the undersides of their wings and belly are pitch black, with clumps of stardust that mimic actual stars. So when you are looking up at them from below, they are practically impossible to spot—unless of course, you know what to look for," Orion explained.

"Had we been on the ground, I never would have noticed," I agreed. "What should I be looking for?"

"If you look closely, you can see a faint trail of stardust streaming from its tail feathers and wing tips," he murmured, coming closer so he could point it out for me.

"I see it." I followed the direction of his finger, and saw that there was indeed a faint glitter of concentrated stardust. I never would have even thought to look for it. After a moment, I became keenly aware that Orion was not moving away again.

"Astrid, I have been meaning to say this for some time now...thank you for saving me. And for taking care of me and the guild when I...while I recovered." He ran a hand through his hair, sending a shower of miniature stars into the air around us.

"I was happy to return the favor." I poked one of the stars, smiling when it twinkled before winking out and dissolving on my skin. I felt the starsteel necklace and rings that Jolene had given me to wear hum in response.

"I mean it," Orion rumbled. "In all honesty, when I lost my father, and then my mother's amulet...I knew it was not true, but a part of me feared no one would stay once they learned I could no longer grant wishes. I hated feeling so...powerless."

I finally met his glowing gaze, and saw the raw emotion there, glimmering under the surface. I put my hand over his where it rested on the railing.

"Orion, none of us followed you because of your mysterious powers. We followed you because you always try to do what is right and help people—with or without magic."

"Thank you." He put his free hand over mine, and I tried not to shiver at the warmth of his skin on mine. "Today's...revelations were quite shocking. Do you think we can trust her?"

"Yes. I suspected she was a witch, but I was still surprised to hear that Adelaide left her coven because of mistreatment," I replied absently. Butterflies had begun fluttering around my insides at his nearness.

"What? You knew? How?" Orion's eyes flew wide, but he kept his hand over mine.

"When we first met, the starsteel ring I wore dispelled the glamour over her eyes, just for a moment. That, combined with her knowledge of herbs I had never seen before, plus Rafe..." I laughed quietly. "I took an educated guess."

Orion sighed. "And you did not mention this because...?"

"At the time, you were...indisposed." Orion winced. "And besides, I wanted to judge her based on her actions, not her heritage. Not every member of a group is joined at the hip with the rest of them." There was a bitter edge to my voice that had become more difficult to hide after I learned the truth from Jolene.

"Like you?" Orion's tone was soft, but the question still startled me. We never spoke of it, so sometimes I forgot that he knew where I was originally from.

I looked away from the questions in his eyes, because the answers hovered on the tip of my tongue. "Like me."

"Astrid, is something wrong? I know this sounds rich coming from me, of all people, but you have been rather distant lately, and with your hair... I appreciate you accompanying me to the Druidlands, but if it is too painful, you can always stay here with Jolene." He lifted his hand from mine to gently turn my face towards his, forcing me to look at him.

"I..." I wanted so badly to confide in him, especially when he was looking at me like that. My eyes dropped to his lips, but I jerked them back to his glowing blue eyes. I knew better than to get my hopes up.

"You know you can tell me anything," he pressed. "Let me be there for you, like you have always been there for me."

My heart sang at the sincerity in his tone, in his eyes. But if I told him the truth, and he tried to save me with magic he did not know how to wield... What if he used up his lifeforce instead? What if the cost of *my* life was *his?*

No, I would not ask that of him. I refused to risk repeating the tragedy that befell his parents. I was simply going to enjoy spending as much time as I could with him.

"I know. I suppose I am just feeling a tad nervous about seeing the home my mother fled," I lied. "But I refuse to stay behind."

"Are you certain—?"

"Orion, look!" I gasped, pointing up at the sea of stars. A shooting star streaked across the darkness, followed closely by a second.

"They almost look like they are running late for something," he joked, but still watched the stars until they flew out of sight.

A sudden thought occurred to me. "Could your mother fly?"

Orion gave me a funny look. "I have no idea." Then he peered over the edge and into the inky darkness below us. "Should I jump and find out?"

I laughed and took his hand, tugging him away from the edge. "Dance with me instead!"

"To what music?" he said with a chuckle, but did not resist.

"To the whistle of the wind—the kind of music the stars dance to."

I pulled him to the center of the deck and guided his free hand to my waist, feeling bold. He was hesitant at first, but to my surprise, Orion took the lead from there. He twirled me around the deck, our footsteps pattering like rain on the wooden boards. I laughed in surprise and delight, humming broken bits of the folk songs that went with this type of dancing.

The star-studded sky formed the most beautiful backdrop, and as we danced and spun I could no longer feel the chill of the cold wind, but my cheeks were pink all the same. It felt like we were performers on a stage, with an audience of stars, winking their applause at us. The constant ache of the curse dulled as I gave this moment my full attention, reveling in this chance to forget our worries and simply enjoy each other's company, the way we used to.

Once we were breathing hard, Orion slowed our lively steps to a smooth waltz—which gave me way too much time to become aware of the warmth of his hand on my waist, and the way the white plumes of our breath mingled in the cold night air.

Of the heat in Orion's gaze when he looked at me.

I glanced away, trying and failing to control my beating heart. I knew he did not think of me *that* way—he never had. Even if remembering the way he had asked who hurt me still sent pleasant shivers down my spine.

A tear of joy and sorrow slipped from my eye when it hit me that this could very well be the last time I was ever alone with him like this. That all of my *maybes* and *somedays* were transforming into *nevers*.

"Tell me," Orion urged. He stilled, raising his hand from my waist to wipe my tears away with his thumb.

"There is something I have wanted to say to you for the longest time," I blurted out, even as I wanted to snatch the words back.

"Oh?" Orion raised an eyebrow.

I hesitated for a moment before plowing on. Jolene was right. I wanted him to know how I felt, before it was too late. When the curse overcame me, I did not want to have any regrets.

"I love you," I whispered with trembling lips.

Orion's beautiful silvery-blue eyes widened as he went still, and he slowly cupped my cheek like it was made of gold. His eyes searched mine before dropping to my lips.

And then, to my complete and utter shock, Orion gently tilted my chin up and kissed me, making my secret wish come true. I cried with joy and sorrow as I caressed his lips with mine, grateful but desperately aching for more time with him, the one thing I knew I could not have.

Orion

I lifted the hem of my tunic to wipe the sweat from my brow after another intensive training session with Jolene, Leo, Noctus, and a few of the crew. Instead of individual sparring, we had been focusing almost entirely on fighting as a group against another group over the last few days, in preparation for the battles to come.

I heard a faint noise, and spotted Astrid's cheeks glowing a lovely shade of pink before she turned her attention back towards her archery practice with Aria.

A grin curved my lips as I let my tunic fall back into place. I had been enjoying every stolen moment I could find with Astrid, even as we drew inevitably closer to our destination. I had never allowed myself to entertain anything other than platonic intentions towards her before. I had feared the consequences, not only of the guild grinding to a halt without her, should things not work out, but also of a relationship where I could never be fully honest and open with her about who I really was.

But now that she knew everything, I had nothing left to hide from her. And losing my father had shown me that spending time with those I cared about was far more important to me than anything else.

The grief from losing both my father and my home was still there, hovering at the edges of my heart and mind, threatening to rush in and smother me again if I was not careful. But each lingering touch and smile from Astrid helped me keep those thoughts and emotions at bay, helped me to continue looking forward to the future, instead of to the past.

Towards that end, I had only become more determined to retake Astoria. I refused to allow the legacy of my parents, the kingdom they gave their lives to, to be tarnished and defiled.

The road ahead would not be an easy one, but I was slowly coming to understand that I did not have to walk it alone.

"Break for lunch!" Jolene called, once she had finished giving Leo a thrashing. Despite his panting, his eyes danced with excitement. He looked more alive than I had ever seen him.

I flashed Astrid an apologetic smile before approaching Jolene. After mulling some ideas over, I was ready to seek her counsel on them.

"Could I speak with you over lunch? I would like to hear your feedback on something." Since she had more practical experience with the customs of other kingdoms than I did, I had a feeling she could provide valuable insight.

"Unfortunately, I already promised to eat with Leo." Jolene smiled as Leo joined us. I blinked in surprise.

"Surely we could spare a few minutes for him," Leo reasoned.

"I was actually hoping to ask the both of you for your thoughts and advice," I hurried to add, when Jolene looked rather doubtful.

"Fine," she sighed, still seeming a tad put-out. "I will have some food brought to my cabin."

Leo winked at me as we followed the pirate belowdecks, and I raised my eyebrows at him. He shrugged casually, but I could tell his smile was genuine. It had been clear that Jolene was interested in him from the start, but I had been surprised to see the stoic soldier so quickly smitten.

We each pulled up a chair around the large desk that occupied one side of the cabin after Jolene carefully removed the large map covering it. Her first mate, Clara, brought three trays of steaming meat pie and set them on the table, and we nodded our thanks.

"So, what is it that you wanted to ask us?" Jolene said around a mouthful of food. I resisted the temptation to grin at the thought of how the pirate and her table manners, or lack thereof, would have been received back at the castle.

"Since both of you have first-hand knowledge of Harland, and to an extent the Druidlands, I wanted to ask for your thoughts on the terms I intend to offer them both as part of an alliance." I folded my hands in front of me, suddenly too nervous to eat.

Jolene and Leo glanced at each other, before Leo gestured for me to continue.

"I have been pondering how a restored Astoria could meet the needs of both peoples, based on what I have heard they lack. For Harland, I was thinking of offering a new trade route through the Druidlands, in addition to our current one by sea. Of course, that is pursuant upon how talks with the druids go." I chuckled drily.

"For the druids, and for Harland, a mutual defense against the incursions of the witches would be the most pressing issue. Astoria could offer a designated supply of starsteel every month, to boost their military might against the magic-wielders, while also increasing their defensive capabilities. And since both of them lie between us and the Desertlands, I doubt either are particularly happy about the hordes of armed tribesmen trespassing through their lands. It is my hope they will be open to returning them to—and keeping them—in the desert."

"Your offer of starsteel will be tempting for Harland." Leo stroked his beard thoughtfully. "The witches strike them most frequently of all, and though wartroot is somewhat effective in keeping them away, it does not offer much protection from their hexes."

"I agree. But the druids may be more...unpredictable. They are a proud people, so you must be careful in your wording. They may interpret offers of aid as an insult, an insinuation that they are incapable of defending their own borders," Jolene mused. "Much will depend on the beliefs of their current King or Queen—if the old king still rules, you may have a much tougher time than you were expecting."

"Have you met this king before?" I questioned, frowning.

Would a ruler really put his own pride before the safety of his people? Their forest was lush in resources, so I had no doubt the tribesmen would begin raiding them once they had fully conquered Astoria.

"Only tales from those who have met him. From what I gathered, King Orwen was a proud traditionalist, who was determined to keep out all outsiders." Jolene scowled.

"And he still reigns?" I knew druids had a considerably longer lifespan than the other races, so it was entirely possible.

"For your sake, I hope not. The last I heard of him was some twenty years ago, and he was far from his prime then. You will have to hope that a new ruler has taken his place."

I nodded slowly. That complicated matters. I would have to hope for the best, but prepare for the worst. At least such a strict traditionalist would already be extremely unhappy with the foreigners traipsing through his territory on the warpath.

"Orion..." Leo began tentatively, his face solemn. "Have you thought about what you will do should either of them demand their wishes to be granted as a condition of alliance?"

I winced. That was the one topic I was still having trouble with.

"I only just learned that I am capable of granting wishes without relying on my mother's amulet—though I have no idea how. There is no one to teach me, and a single mistake could cost me my life—as it did my mother's." I dropped my face to my hands, rubbing my tired eyes.

I felt Leo place a hand on my shoulder. "It is a heavy burden you carry, son."

I closed my eyes, fighting back the wave of emotion that swelled up like a tidal wave when he called me *son*. I wondered longingly what advice my own father would have given me.

"Chin up, princeling," Jolene said brusquely. "The important thing is that you already have all that you need. There is no need to mention *why* you cannot grant wishes immediately—simply promise them a set number of granted wishes in the future, if that is something they demand."

"Brilliant! That way, you can say that any wishes will depend on whether the other party holds up their end of the bargain." Leo clapped me on the back encouragingly.

I finally scrubbed my hands over my face and raised my eyes to see the two of them smiling at me. I gave them a weak smile in return. I felt lucky to have met them both.

"I am very glad I asked." I had needed someone to listen to me talk, if only so I could sort through my own thoughts properly.

"Now, hurry up and eat before your food gets cold," Jolene scolded gently.

"I will, thanks." I took a bite of the meat pie, savoring its warmth and rich flavor. Food, I had discovered, was one thing the pirate never seemed to skimp on.

"Oh, and I am glad to see Astrid so happy these days," Jolene added, a little too casually. "I expect you to pay close attention to her, and to always treat her right."

I choked on my food, some of it going down the wrong pipe in my surprise. My eyes watered as I coughed, and Leo's big, booming laugh rang out as he pounded me on the back.

"I could say the same about Leo," I fired back.

Now it was the pirate's turn to sputter. Jolene's cheeks turned pink, but Leo only laughed all the harder. I grinned, and dug into my pie.

If only we could spend every meal like this. But there was a storm on the horizon, so I would have to content myself with appreciating these little moments of tranquility as they came. Thunder rumbled ominously in the distance, but for now, I could ignore the coming tempest.

Astrid

"This is impossible!" Aria cried in frustration.

"This is good practice!" I retorted.

I drew the bowstring back to my ear, lined up my shot, aiming to the left of my true target, and fired. My arrow zipped through the tumultuous air, and the tip buried itself in the bullseye.

I turned to Aria, who was gaping at me, her own bow held forgotten at her side. "See?"

"How did you do that?! The wind keeps blowing mine off course!" She bounced on the balls of her feet excitedly. She reminded me of Nova when she did that.

My smile slipped a tad at that thought. Even with the extra time my daily intake of stardust was buying me, I could feel the curse eating away at my magic every day. Our hurried goodbyes at the guildhouse might have been my last glimpse of the fiery redhead and her faithful friend, Castor.

"A skilled archer can shoot in any weather." I turned my gaze on the dark and angry storm clouds that lined the horizon.

We had kept ahead of the tempest for most of the day, but now that sunset was painting the sky a stunning hue of red and gold, it appeared the storm had no intention of letting us escape its wrathful embrace. I shivered. I had hoped we would have smooth sailing all the way to the Druidlands, but that seemed like wishful thinking now.

The most I had been able to do was to keep Aria distracted with some more archery practice. The distraction was good for me too—it kept my thoughts on the present, instead of my future—or lack thereof.

"How much do I have to practice before I can do that too?" Aria looked down, fidgeting with her bow.

I ruffled her hair. "Only one way to find out."

She stuck her tongue out at me, and I laughed. My gaze drifted across the deck, and I noticed I was not the only person who kept glancing at the threatening clouds. But then my eyes snagged on Adelaide, whose unnatural red eyes were pinned on Orion.

Unease flickered through me like a shadow. I had noticed her watching him over the last few days, but I tried to brush aside my suspicions. Still, her words about how witches desired him for his powers rang in my ears. Adelaide had escaped from her coven for a reason; there was no way she harbored any ill intentions like they would. Right?

Orion glanced over at me, and when he saw that I was watching him, he broke into a wide grin. I smiled as he walked over, admiring the way his dampened tunic clung to his muscular frame. He took my hand as if it were the most natural thing in the world. My shiver had nothing to do with the chill of the wind.

"How goes practice?" he rumbled.

"Astrid is amazing! She can hit the target even with this strong wind! I can barely even get near it," Aria reported.

Orion smiled warmly at her. "With enough practice, I have no doubt you will be able to do that too."

"That is exactly what Astrid said! Did you two coordinate in secret or something?" Aria complained. She crossed her little arms over her chest in mock indignation.

"We did not. But perhaps we should." His light blue eyes deepened into pools of cobalt when they met mine.

I looked down, too happy for words. I still had no clue how to react when he looked at me like that. When I looked up again, I noticed Jolene winking at me. It seemed I had *her* to thank for Orion's newfound courage.

A flash of lightning split the twilight sky, followed quickly by the ominous rumbling of thunder. A ferocious gust of wind rocked the starship, testing the balance we had been honing over the last week.

"All hands! Batten the hatches! Raise the sails!" Jolene roared over the howling of the wind. "The storm is upon us!"

"Aria, take the starbird inside and make sure it does not fly into the storm," I ordered. She immediately took down the target and grabbed the precious bird from Jolene before racing belowdecks.

"I will help secure the ropes. Please, get belowdecks as well." Orion gave my hand a squeeze, but refused to budge until I reluctantly agreed. It made me happy he was so worried about me.

I watched for a moment as Orion ran over to help Leo secure one of the huge canvas sails on the mainmast, their muscles straining against the force of the wind. A flash of lightning lit up the darkening sky again, and I could feel the booming thunder shaking the worn wood beneath my feet. The sky opened up, drenching me within seconds. We were well and truly in the midst of the tempest now.

"Let me help!" Adelaide cried, drawing my attention as I moved towards the narrow stairway that led belowdecks.

"No!" came the swift reply.

The witch seemed to be trying to use her magic to secure the heavy chain of the anchor, but the crewmate was having none of it. She glared suspiciously at the girl and her wolf, mistrustful of a magic that was known to exclusively cause others pain.

A sudden gust sent the deck tilting, and I raced towards Rafe when I saw him scrabbling for purchase on the rain-slick wood. He slid several feet before I reached him. The whites of his eyes were showing all the way around, telling me how scared the big wolf was. Still, when I tried to tug him to safety, he shook his head and clawed his way back towards Adelaide.

"I can do this for you!" Adelaide insisted, as her hands glowed purple. Instinctively, I knew I was seeing her magic.

"Cast a hex on me, witch, and I will gut you where you stand," spat the sailor. Her hand drifted closer to her cutlass.

"Adelaide, they know what they are doing—we would only get in the way if we tried to help!" I grabbed her wrist, but was unprepared for the sudden pain that stole my breath away.

I released her wrist and quickly stepped back, silently cursing my stupidity. Of course the curse would become more active if my skin touched such a deep wellspring of magic it could feed off of. I blinked rapidly in an attempt to clear the darkness lurking at the edges of my vision. If I fainted now, I may very well be blown off the ship!

"Astrid? Are you hurt?" Adelaide asked, taking a step towards me.

I took a step back to maintain my distance, but immediately regretted it at the flash of hurt that crossed the witch's face. "We have to get Rafe belowdecks—before he loses his grip on the wood and gets blown off the ship! But he refuses to leave your side, so—"

I staggered as the deck tilted again. I trapped the wolf against the mainmast, wincing at the splinters that dug into my fingers as I held onto the rough wood with everything I had. I squeezed my eyes shut as I tried to hold on, but the deck just kept tilting farther and farther. My fingers began to slip and panic closed my throat.

Was I about to be swept into the empty sky?

I knew I had little time left, but I simply was not ready yet! If I lost my grip, both Rafe and I were goners. I knew this day would come, but now that it was potentially here...I wanted nothing more than to see another starfall with Orion. To tease Nova, teach Castor, play with Estelle, laugh around the dinner table with Sirius and Noctus and even Celeste.

"Astrid! Hang on!" Orion cried.

I clenched my jaw, mustering every ounce of strength I had left to fight against the wind and the storm, to defy the ever-increasing angle of the deck. I yelled in pain as my fingernails bit into the rough wood and the wood bit back, the muscles in my fingers and arms trembling from the strain. And then my foot slipped on the slick floor.

"I got you!" Orion grunted in my ear, just as I lost my grip completely.

His strong arms wrapped around me, his calloused hands grabbing onto the mainmast. His chest pressed against my back, securely trapping both me and Rafe against the wooden pillar. The deck continued tilting until we were almost vertical, and despite his knuckles turning white, Orion kept us safe.

With a great, creaking groan that made the deck shudder beneath our feet, the starship righted itself, rocking in the opposite direction before settling back into its proper position. Orion finally released his death-grip on the mast. I staggered from exhaustion, leaning back into Orion, who wrapped his arms around me. I rested my head on his heaving chest, terrified by how close I had come to plummeting into the empty air.

A tear slipped down my face, mingling with the icy cold rain. I had thought I had resigned myself to my fate, that I was prepared to face the end. But when death stared back at me just now, I had desperately searched for a way out. I had clung to life, knowing there was still so much more I wanted to do, to experience.

And that, more than anything else, terrified me.

Had I been giving up on life too easily? Would it really be a waste of my precious time to look for a cure?

I looked up at Orion's face, at the hard set of his jaw and the way the rain had plastered his dark hair to his forehead. If I told him the truth, what would he do? Could he handle looking for a way to save me and his kingdom at the same time? If he had to choose between us, what would his choice be? And why was I so afraid to find out?

His eyes met mine, and he smiled just for me. He pressed a kiss to the top of my wet hair as he rubbed some warmth back into my arms. "Are you all right?"

"I am now," I rasped.

I looked around to see that Jolene had kept Leo from falling, and I spotted Noctus tangled in some netting high above us. Members of the crew were returning to the deck as if nothing had happened, as if this were just another storm to them. I supposed it was. A life-threatening situation for us was simply another day at work for them.

A bark of alarm startled me, and I looked down to see Rafe tugging at Orion's pant leg. He whined deep in his throat, and nearly pulled Orion off his feet in his frenzy.

"What the...quit it, Rafe!" Orion shouted to be heard over the roar of the wind as he staggered forward.

I looked in the direction the wolf was trying to take him, and noticed a pair of hands just barely holding onto the side of the ship. The only person Rafe would be this frantic about was...

"Adelaide!" I cried as I rushed over to the railing, Orion just a step behind me.

Sure enough, the witch was just barely holding onto the edge, but her fingers kept slipping because of the torrential rain. I immediately grabbed one of her hands, with Orion grabbing the other. Rafe dug into the back of Orion's tunic with his teeth, clearly trying to help.

"Can you get a foothold?!" Orion demanded as we started to pull her up.

"No, there is nothing there." For some reason, Adelaide did not look nearly as bothered as I would have expected for someone dangling over the edge of a starship.

Why was she so calm?

Another sudden gust tilted the deck in the most unhelpful direction, causing us to have to brace our feet against the side wall of the ship. Lightning struck, the bright light catching on the star-shaped pendant that had worked its way out of Orion's tunic. It dangled in front of Adelaide's face, and her red eyes tracked its every movement.

I gritted my teeth as the curse licked at the edges of my mind. The malevolent magic could sense the reservoir of Adelaide's magic through our skin-on-skin contact, and it took all my willpower to keep it from siphoning off of her as well.

As the ship rocked back the other way, we used that momentum to haul Adelaide over the side to safety. She tumbled onto the deck, and Rafe immediately began nuzzling her, checking for injuries. She idly patted his back, but her eyes never left the pendant.

"Are you all right?" I crouched next to her, scanning for any injuries as well. Other than some scrapes on her palms, she seemed to be unhurt.

"I am fine." She finally tore her eerie eyes away from the necklace to look at me. She appeared surprised that I had asked. "...Thank you."

"Is everyone accounted for?" Jolene called over the wind as she came over to scan our faces.

"Just barely," Orion muttered, rubbing his undoubtedly sore hands.

"Good. Now get yourselves belowdecks before you ruin my clean record," she ordered.

"What record?" Orion offered Adelaide a hand, and after a moment of hesitation, she took it and allowed him to haul her to her feet. Rafe walked circles around her like an anxious mother hen.

"My record of not losing any of my passengers overboard," she roared. "Now get your rubbery landlubber legs belowdecks already!"

Astrid

The next day, we all pitched in to repair the damage from the storm. It had certainly been a rough night, and no one had gotten so much as a wink of sleep with the ship pitching to and fro. At least when we were ensconced belowdecks, there was no risk of losing someone to the turbulent skies below.

In contrast to the dark and stormy night, the dawn had been a spectacular masterpiece of brilliant reds, pinks, and baby blues. The gales had finally died down to a gentle breeze, and the wisps of clouds that remained were fluffy and white. It would have been perfect, if not for the sight it revealed below us on the horizon.

The great and sprawling forest the druids called home was finally in view, marking the approaching end of our journey through the sky. We would reach it either tonight or tomorrow morning. Dread curled in the pit of my stomach like a viper, and a throb of pain from the curse reminded me of the danger that awaited me below.

"Tired?" Orion asked sympathetically. He joined me where I worked at mending a tear in one of the minor sails.

"Not as tired as you, I imagine." I glanced down at the bits of tar still coating his fingers. He, Leo and Noctus had been commandeered into patching some leaks in the hull.

He gave a quiet chuckle. "I can manage." He draped an arm over my shoulders, but was careful not to get any tar on my clothes.

"Should we delay our meeting with the druids until tomorrow morning?" I leaned into him, my fingers stilling as I rested my tired eyes for just a moment.

"That might be a good idea. A few hours of sleep might help with our negotiating skills." He yawned, and it was my turn to chuckle.

I smiled with relief. "I doubt we would be taken very seriously looking like this, anyways."

"True."

"I was surprised the storm did not blow us further off course." I had secretly hoped it would.

"Thanks to the captain. She was at the helm all night, steering us through the storm."

I glanced over to where Jolene was currently securing the ropes, her hands coated with tar. "I had no idea."

"She is a hard worker, and incredibly tough and loyal to her crew. Honestly, if the negotiations go well, and I can retake

Astoria, I was thinking of hiring her on as an Admiral of a royal starfleet."

I looked at him in surprise. "You plan to establish an Astorian navy?"

He nodded solemnly. "It was foolish to have only a small core of knights and guards on call. If my father had created a standing army and navy, Astoria might not have fallen so easily."

I set down my needle and thread so I could turn and give him a peck on the cheek, before wrapping my arms around him. "I am proud of you for facing your father's shortcomings in order to learn from them."

Orion pressed a kiss to my hair that made me want to melt. "Thank you for not giving up on me, even when *I* did."

"I will never give up on you." I leaned into his touch, savoring his scent, his warmth, his everything.

We stood like that for a time, simply enjoying each other's company and delaying the inevitable. If I could simply stay in his arms like this forever, I would ask for nothing more.

"I see you have abandoned us to our labor." Leo materialized beside us, making me jump.

"They keep getting worse," Noctus teased with a rare smile. "I can hardly stand to watch."

I blushed.

"Some tar to the eyes might solve that problem." Orion wiggled his tar-streaked fingers in Noctus' face in mock threat.

Noctus stepped out of reach, and looked both confused and delighted when Orion continued to chase him, and they both wound up doing some hand-to-hand sparring. Apparently, they were not as tired as they had let on. I smiled to myself when I saw Aria join in on their fun, and I even spotted Adelaide smiling at their antics from where she watched.

"Boys," Leo muttered with a disapproving scowl. But his lips twitched upwards at the corners.

"Do not lie—I can tell you wish to join them," Jolene purred as she joined us.

Leo scoffed. "I am far too old for such tomfoolery."

"Is that so? How unfortunate." As Leo turned red and made a choking sound, Jolene turned to me. "I would like to see you and Orion in my quarters tomorrow at dawn, before you depart."

"I will let him know...whenever he is done."

I wiped the sleep from my eyes as Orion and I were ushered into Jolene's cabin. She held her finger to her lips, indicating we should not speak. I glanced at Orion, and he shrugged, just as confused as I was. Why was the pirate acting so suspiciously? What needed to be kept secret from her own crew?

We watched silently as she locked and bolted the door behind us, and then went to each curtain and fastened them closed, plunging her cozy quarters into darkness. Only a faint strip of the dawn light snuck through the very edges of the thick black curtains.

Once our eyes adjusted, Jolene gestured for us to join her over by one of the two doors that flanked the main entrance. She paused outside of the one I had assumed led to additional storage, and with a grand flourish flung the door open wide.

My jaw dropped at what I saw. Orion burst out laughing, even as Jolene beamed with pride.

Beyond the door, illuminated by an expensive starlight lantern, was the most extravagant closet I had ever laid eyes on. It was the size of a small room, large enough for at least three people to stand comfortably inside. The top shelf was stuffed with all kinds of hats, some studded with gems, others with colorful feathers stuck jauntily onto one side. They ranged in size from small berets to wide-brimmed sun bonnets, and bits of satin ribbons hung over the edge of the shelf.

Below the hats, dresses, frilly blouses, and voluminous skirts in every color imaginable hung from racks. I saw bright pink dresses covered in lace and frills, royal blue skirts with tiny crystals sewn into the hem, and satin blouses in the purest of ivory with pearl-studded bodices all packed together, in no discernable order.

Boots, sandals, and dainty, jewel-encrusted ballroom slippers were arranged in compartments on the floor, the wood frame bolted into the walls to prevent them from clattering around during voyages. Most of them looked like they had hardly even been worn. There was also a small, locked chest in the corner, with pink, red, and blue flowers painted across the top. Above it, secured to the wall, was a long and narrow floor-length mirror, the kind that I had only ever seen in the homes of wealthy merchants.

"We need to do something about..." she gestured to our clothes. *"That.* You want to make a good first impression on your potential allies and look like a prince and a diplomat, not like drowned rats."

"You make a good point." Orion ran a hand through his mussed hair sheepishly.

"But, needless to say, if you tell a single soul about my secret, I will have you tossed overboard. Understood?" She pointed her finger at us both, her tone so serious I could not tell if she was joking.

"We promise not to tell. Your secret is safe with us," I reassured her.

"Good. Now, where did I put them...?" Jolene mumbled to herself, as she rummaged through her closet.

After a minute, she returned with a bundle of clothes in her arms and a pair of large, polished leather boots gripped in one hand. She shoved the bundle at Orion, who hastily grabbed the items before they could fall.

"Go through the other door to wash yourself and change into these. And make sure to tidy up that scraggly little beard you have there." Jolene shooed him away from the closet and towards the door that led to her private bathing chamber. He looked baffled and bemused, but obeyed nonetheless.

"And now, for the main event." Once he was gone, Jolene turned to me, a sparkle in her eye that made me a tad nervous. "We are going to find you the perfect dress!"

The next hour was a whirlwind of activity. Jolene had me try on dress after dress, and I started to feel like a child's doll being dressed up in matching outfits. But when I imagined that this was the sort of thing a mother might do with her daughter... Well, I found myself enjoying the process a little more.

"Twirl," Jolene instructed, her critical eye roving over the burgundy fabric and all the bits of lace that fluttered at the shoulders and hem when I moved. "No, this one is not quite right either."

"Agreed." I scanned the seemingly endless racks of dresses, my eye catching on a gauzy teal one I had yet to notice, so I pointed it out to her. "Can I try that one?"

"But of course!" She handed it to me, and it was the work of a moment for me to slip out of the old one and into the new. As I buttoned up the side, Jolene set a pair of sturdy slippers in front of me. They were made out of soft leather, and embroidered on the top with little green and blue flowers.

"Oh, this might be the one," Jolene breathed. She put her hands on my shoulders and moved me in front of the mirror, brushing my hair aside so it cascaded over my shoulder.

The gauzy sleeves fluttered elegantly around my shoulders. The floral-patterned bodice hugged my chest and waist and flared out slightly at my hips, a few crystals winking in the lantern light. A gauzy layer of fabric lay on top of the thicker teal skirt, and extended past the hem. The dress looked like it had come straight out of the pages of a fairy tale, as if it were the dress of a forest nymph.

"It still needs a little something, however." Jolene retrieved a key from where it hung around her neck like a necklace, and bent to unlock the small chest in the corner.

I gasped when she turned around, holding out a necklace that glimmered with sparkling aquamarine and sapphire gemstones, and gently placed it around my neck.

"There. I cannot wait to see Orion's expression when he sees you like this. I bet his jaw will drop!" Jolene giggled girlishly, her emerald eyes lit up with delight.

"Jolene, I...I cannot accept this." My fingers fluttered over the precious stones at my neck. I could hardly begin to estimate their value.

"Oh, hogwash. You can and you will. But if you feel the need to repay me in some way..." she trailed off, giving me the side-eye.

"What can I do for you?" I hoped it was something I could manage.

"Enjoy every moment you can with your prince. I often wish I had not taken for granted the time I had with my beloved husband and daughter." Her eyes softened, even as her voice thickened with emotion. She took my hands tenderly. "And please, if you refuse to share your secret with Orion, promise me you will seek out the druid who aided your mother. She may know more about that despicable curse, even potentially how to undo it."

A lump rose in my throat, and I squeezed her hands. "I will."

Jolene cleared her throat. "Now, shall we go and see his reaction?"

I nodded eagerly, and she gave me a warm smile.

When I cautiously emerged from the closet, Orion was leaning casually against the wall, gazing down at the star-shaped pendant he held in his hand. The dark jacket and pants Jolene had given him looked like they had been tailored to fit, and despite the ruffled cravat on it, the white tunic suited him well. And with his starsword strapped to his hip, his dark hair slicked back and his goatee trimmed, he looked every inch the prince—no, the king—that he was.

He looked up as I emerged, his lips parting in surprise as his blue eyes drank me in. The flowing skirts whispered around my legs as I moved into the room, and even in the dim light, I had no doubt the gems were glittering at my throat. The heat in his gaze melted my core, and I looked down shyly.

Orion pushed off the wall and held out his hand, and after a moment of hesitation, I placed my hand in his. He brought it to his lips and pressed a kiss to the back of my hand, sending tingles of delight up my arm.

"My lady," he murmured, his eyes pinning me to the spot. "You look beautiful."

I flushed what must have been a bright crimson, and Orion grinned. For a moment, I could pretend that we really were in a fairy tale. So long as we stayed inside this little room, floating in the sky, we could be a prince and a princess without a care in the world.

"And you look very handsome...Sterling," I tried out his real name, its form unfamiliar on my tongue.

His grin widened, and he bowed slightly. I suddenly became very much aware that Jolene was hovering, slowly inching closer and closer. My ears grew warm, and I could practically feel her beaming at us.

He offered me his arm. "Are you ready?"

I mustered up a smile and slipped my arm through his. "Ready as I will ever be."

After some light teasing and whistles from the crew and the others, Orion went to give final instructions to Leo for his negotiations with Harland while I said my goodbyes to Aria and then to Jolene.

"Please take care of yourselves." My fingers fidgeted with the fabric of my beautiful dress.

"You take care of yourself too, little star." The ghost of a smile appeared on the captain's wind-chapped lips, and she gripped my shoulder in a rare show of affection outside her cabin. "And make sure to take plenty of stardust." She handed me a hefty pouch of the precious powder, and I took it gratefully.

I gave her my best smile, wishing I could stay with her longer. A twinge of melancholy shivered through me at the realization that this may well be one of the last times I saw the captain, if the curse continued progressing at its current rate.

But I shoved that thought to the back of my mind. Dwelling on my fate would do no one any good. I was surprised when Adelaide's wolf brushed up against my side, as if sensing that I needed to be comforted. I stroked his soft head, and he wagged his tail in response.

I wondered again at the strangely familiar magic I felt from the animal. Could he sense the twisted magic within me, as well? Perhaps he could sense that I was dying, as I had heard some animals could.

Instead of answering the captain directly, I said simply, "I will look forward to seeing you and Leo once we have both secured our alliances, then."

"I will do my best to help him, and to be waiting for you just beyond the forest, to fly you back to Astoria. And tell that rascal of a guildmaster to keep practicing—or I will have the pleasure of trouncing him in a sparring match when next we meet." Captain Jolene propped her hands on her hips and gave a predatory grin.

I just laughed. "I will be sure to tell him."

"Good girl." She gave my shoulder one last squeeze as Orion rejoined us. "Off with you then—and may the stars be with you."

Noctus, Adelaide, Rafe, Orion and I clambered into the lifeboat, where one of her crew waited to ferry us down to the edge of the forest from where the main starship hovered in the air.

As we began our descent towards the forest, my chin quivered, and I tried not to dwell on the fact that, should my grandfather still be alive, he might decide to finish what his curse had started by the end of the day.

Orion

I stared into the impenetrable depths of the foreboding forest, knowing I was unlikely to spot a druid until we were well within the trees, but searching nonetheless. It spread out like an undulating sea of green before us, the trunks seeming to grow taller as we floated gently towards the ground.

Astrid was stiff as a board beside me, and Noctus kept checking his weapons, telling me I was far from the only one who was worried. Even Adelaide, who was normally so calm, kept fidgeting. I had debated sending her with Leo to Harland, but given that country's history with witches, even leaving her on the ship would be risky. I just had to hope we could convince the druids to allow her entry with us, if I vouched for her character.

But what if what I had to offer was not enough? Late last night, I had stood out on the deck, bathing in the starlight and trying to replicate what I had done that night to save Rigel. But no matter how hard I tried to access that well of power, it remained beyond my reach. Like Leo and Jolene suggested, I would have to try to stall for time if it were wishes they wanted from me.

The gentle thump of the lifeboat's hull touching down on the thick grass jolted me from my thoughts. The Druidlands spread out in an endless line before me. From the maps I had studied, I knew that the trees stretched from the sea to the mountains of the Varlett Witchlands. It was a formidable natural barrier that completely cut Astoria off from the Rocklands and the Desertlands further south.

"This is as far as I can take you," our guide informed me. "Best of luck in there. We will try to return for you as swiftly as possible."

"Thank you." Before I stepped out of the boat, I rummaged in my pocket and withdrew my spare starsteel watch, and handed it over. "I nearly forgot—please give this to Captain Jolene."

"Understood."

I took a steeling breath and stepped out of the lifeboat, offering a hand to Astrid and then Adelaide as they exited as well. Noctus kept his eyes on the forest, guarding my back, and once Rafe had jumped out of the boat, it began to rise once more.

"Long live Astoria! Long live Prince Sterling!" The pirate saluted me with an impish grin as she rose out of sight. Even if today's reception did not go as planned, I knew I could count on at least one pirate ship to ally with me.

I walked to the edge of the forest, my friends walking beside me. I paused at the invisible line where the forest began.

"Though darkness falls..."

"Still the stars find their way."

And with that, I stepped into the Druidlands.

The towering trees made me feel small, and although I could hear birds calling, the sound seemed muted, somehow. A curious mist swirled around our legs as we walked. It was far quieter than the woods I had once played in, and I felt reluctant to disturb the silence. Everyone else must have felt the same, since no one spoke.

My heart pounded in my ears, and I half-expected a druid patrol to leap out at us at any moment. I glanced at Rafe, and although he seemed alert, his hackles were not raised. I took that as a sign that he sensed no threats in the immediate area.

As we continued walking deeper, my pulse slowly began to calm. The few patches of sunlight that filtered through the thick canopy overhead helped to light the way and ease my fears of a hidden attacker. Hopefully, the druids would question us before launching an attack.

Eventually, after what felt like more than an hour or two of walking, I began to wonder how we were going to find these mysterious druids. Were they spread so thin because of the tribesmen that they had no patrols on their border with Astoria? If no one spotted us, would we be able to wander into one of their villages? What if we simply walked in circles until we became too exhausted to continue?

Just as I was beginning to worry, Rafe growled low in his throat. Noctus immediately drew his blades, but I held out a hand to stay him as a patrol of druids emerged from between two thick trees in front of us. The two male druids each rode a massive elk, with the one in the front brandishing a spear at us while the other had drawn his bow, an arrow already nocked to the string.

Their appearances were consistent with what I had expected; their flaxen hair hung down to their waists, and their emerald-green eyes were narrowed with suspicion and disgust. They wore clothes that were colored to help them blend into their forest surroundings, and a few elegant pieces of jewelry winked at their temples and pointed ears.

"Halt, trespassers!" The druid's cold eyes scanned us quickly, but a sneer curled his lip when his eyes settled on Adelaide and Rafe. "A witch! What trickery is this?!"

He leveled his spear at Adelaide, causing Rafe to jump in front of her protectively. The witch herself looked largely unconcerned, but I could feel my heart begin to pound. We were not off to a great start.

"Adelaide has defected from her coven, and comes with us now not as a witch, but as a diplomatic delegate," I hurried to say, stepping forward. I waved a hand at Rafe behind my back, hoping he would understand my signal to back down.

"Delegates from where?" The male inspected me more closely, though I noticed his eyes kept flickering to Astrid, for some reason. "What kingdom would be so bold as to send three magic-wielders and a human to Sylvaine?"

I blinked. *Three* magic wielders? Was he counting Rafe to arrive at that number?

"I am Prince Sterling Astoria, and I have come personally to speak with your leader on a matter of great importance," I said with as much dignity as I could muster.

"Last we heard, the Woman-King ruled the north now." The spear lowered a fraction.

"The tribeswoman of whom you speak has certainly caused some trouble. I am sure the druids have also encountered...issues, with the number of tribesmen passing through Sylvaine in recent months." I did my best to keep my tone light and even, without outright lying.

My father had once shared with me that druids had the uncanny ability to tell truth from lie as it was spoken, perhaps thanks to their sensitive hearing. I was not sure how accurate that tale was, but I decided it would be safer to stick to as much of the truth as I could until I ascertained the verity of that claim for myself.

The druid withdrew his spear, but did not bow or show deference. After sharing a look with his fellow druid, he finally said, "There is truth to your statement. I am Raiden, and this is Birken. We will escort you to Pyrcairn."

"Your assistance is appreciated." I hid my relief. We had successfully passed the first obstacle. But the real test was only just beginning.

Raiden turned his elk around—without using any bridle or other signal that I could discern. Was he using his wild magic to communicate with the animal?

Raiden glanced over his shoulder. "Birken will follow behind. Needless to say, should the witch or anyone else move to attack, they and the rest of you will be culled."

My gaze hardened, but I nodded curtly. "That will not be necessary."

"I should hope not." Raiden looked forward once more as his elk began to stride forward, its long legs carrying him easily over the thick undergrowth that we had to navigate through.

Birken indeed waited until we had all passed before falling in behind us. I could feel the druid's eyes burning into the back of my head, but tried not to show any outward reaction. Astrid stayed close to my side, and I could tell Noctus remained tense and alert.

We spoke little as we followed the druid through the forest, except to warn each other of hidden roots or tricky brambles. No one wanted to misspeak and cause our guides to become our enemies. I, at least, had a general idea of where we were headed.

I knew Pyrcairn was located not too far from the border, but closer to the sea than the mountains. Loch Glaen sat just south of it, above Cailleach, with Allanon located on the eastern coast, and Daegon acting as their primary line of defense against the witches in the western mountains. Pyrcairn, the village hidden in the trees, had served as the home of the Druid King for as long as anyone could remember.

So far, few outsiders had seen Pyrcairn, or any of their other villages, and lived to tell the tale. Hopefully, our visit would change that.

"Careful." I steadied Astrid as she stumbled on a rock. We had been walking for at least an hour, but as I peered into her face, I realized she was far too pale, her breathing too fast and shallow.

"Thanks." She smiled up at me weakly.

"Raiden! My companions need to rest for a moment." I set my shoulders as the druid glanced at us disinterestedly.

He sighed. "There is a clearing up ahead."

I helped Astrid forward to a fallen log where she could catch her breath. While the druids were not known for their hospitality, forcing a prince and his delegation to walk through a pathless forest at midday was more than a little disrespectful.

Rafe lay panting in the shade beside Adelaide, whose dark hair was plastered to her forehead. Noctus discreetly wiped at his brow, his modest dark clothes sticking to his lean but muscular frame. The clothes Jolene had given us, while very nice, were not designed for hikes. I had taken off my embroidered jacket as soon as we started walking, but the pant legs were streaked with dirt and a couple of tiny tears now. Astrid's dress looked only mildly better.

"Drink more water." I offered my own canteen to Astrid, and she took it gratefully.

Now that I looked closer, when had so much of her hair turned black? I could have sworn it was a lighter brown just this morning—there was no way she could have dyed it while we were walking. Rafe kept glancing at her, as if he could sense something I could not. An idea sparked, and I reached for the magic that always seemed to dwell just out of reach within me. Not to use it, but to remind myself of its unique, tingling sensation.

If I focused, I could detect a similar sensation emanating from Adelaide and Rafe. Now that I was searching for it, I could feel the wild magic of our druid guides. But beside me, I could sense in Astrid a magic that held a whisper of foulness, of rot.

I glanced at her in alarm. What did that sensation mean? Normally I would ask Adelaide, but I did not think it wise to draw more attention to her.

"Are you...feeling all right?" I asked Astrid.

She stiffened, so slightly that I almost missed it. "Simply tired. It has been some time since I did so much walking."

"Of course." But it had only been a week or two since she had been traversing the streets of Astoria with ease. My sense of alarm grew.

"We are not far from Pyrcairn. If we continue now, we should reach it before the sun reaches its zenith," Birken hinted none too subtly.

"Can you go on?" I asked Astrid quietly.

She nodded, but I sensed her hesitation.

"Here." I stood and offered her my arm to help her up. When she went to withdraw, I held tightly onto her. "Lean on me. Or would you rather I carried you?"

"She may ride with me if that will increase our pace," Raiden grudgingly offered.

I checked with Astrid, and when she did not argue, said, "That would be ideal. Thank you."

After helping Astrid up onto the elk in front of Raiden, we continued our march. Just as the druid had said, after almost another hour of walking, I began to see curious structures in the trees. Bridges constructed of wood and vines connected houses that seemed to be built into the trees themselves. Copious amounts of jewel-toned flowers spilled from hanging baskets and window boxes, their petals floating lazily down to the loamy forest floor. Butterflies of all shapes and sizes fluttered around them, dancing through the air like the most graceful of dancers.

A bird called, but when Raiden gave an answering cry, I realized that had been a challenge call. I craned my neck to look up at the trees around us, and sure enough, spotted a sentry perched high on a sturdy branch.

"Welcome to Pyrcairn." Raiden gestured grandly as we entered a massive clearing.

A palatial weeping willow tree stood in the center, a massive dwelling nestled at its base. More buildings and dwellings surrounded it, one section appearing to be reserved for shops, and another for homes and stables. Moss-covered bark served as the roofs, and I saw giant toadstools being used as steps or seats by the druids.

The people here were just as strange as their dwellings. Most wore loose-fitting clothes whose colors matched the dark umber of the tree bark or the viridian green of the grass and leaves. Many of them either rode or were accompanied by some sort of animal companion, such as an elk like our guides, or a small bird or monkey that could ride on their shoulders. All were rather tall, and all had the same golden hair and vivid blue or green eyes.

And all of them stopped to stare at us as we entered.

Fortunately, our guides continued towards the largest dwelling at the base of the willow tree, and none of the druids came up to us. That certainly did not stop them from whispering, though.

Raiden and Birken dismounted near the grand, carved wooden doors at the front, where two more armed druids stood guard.

"You dare bring outsiders to Pyrcairn?!" The guard slammed his spear on the ground angrily.

"And a witch, no less! Raiden, have you lost your senses?" The second sneered at Adelaide.

"We bring the Prince of Astoria and his diplomats to see the queen," Raiden replied calmly, as if he had been expecting such accusations.

Queen? Did that mean the old king Jolene had warned us about had indeed stepped down? Hope rose in my chest. Even though I was the one who had planned all of this, I was only just beginning to believe things would truly work out.

I stepped forward, suddenly grateful to have Raiden and Birken on my side. "There are matters of great importance I wish to discuss with your queen, matters pertaining to the current and future safety of both Astoria and Sylvaine."

The guards eyed me skeptically. I stood tall and proud, falling back on the etiquette my teachers had drilled into me over a lifetime of studies in the castle. I met their gazes evenly, doing my best to appear neither haughty nor nervous.

"Show them to the reception room," the spear-wielding guard eventually said. "But do not let the witch or the other one out of your sight."

I was relieved, but beginning to believe the druids had no concept of etiquette or hospitality. I supposed *I* was the foolish one, for expecting such niceties from a people who lived among the trees, cut off from the rest of the continent.

"Understood." Raiden led us through the large doors that the guards opened for us, revealing a grand entryway.

I nodded to the guards, who did not deign to return the gesture. I felt Astrid press into my side, trembling from either nerves or exhaustion. I looped her arm through mine, so I could support her weight.

The hallways we walked down and the rooms we passed all had warm sunlight filtering through the skylights in the ceilings, providing plenty of light to illuminate the exquisite carvings that adorned nearly every wooden surface. Most featured various aspects of nature, from plants and animals to the druids themselves.

Everywhere I looked, nature was on display. Bouquets of flowers brightened every corner, and paintings lined every wall. Unlike in my own castle, I saw no suits of armor, no stonework, and no ceramics. The only glass I saw comprised the numerous skylights.

Raiden led us to a circular room that contained a number of comfortable chairs and couches. Each held pillows woven from dried grasses, instead of animal hide, and stuffed with downy feathers.

"I will alert the queen to your presence and request, but I cannot guarantee an audience." He gestured for us to sit before he left the room. Birken took up position by the open doorway, his blue eyes watching our every move.

I helped Astrid to sit down, Adelaide choosing a seat to the side. Rafe curled up at her feet, but his ears remained pricked forward alertly. Noctus continued to stand, his muscles loose but ready as he stared back at Birken.

But to my surprise, no more than a few minutes had passed before we heard two sets of footsteps racing towards us. A frantic druid burst into the room with an anxious Raiden hovering behind her. Her waist-length flaxen hair was braided intricately down her back, standing out against the deep emerald green of her elegant dress. Crystals hung from her long, pointed ears, and a golden circlet graced her brow. Vivid turquoise eyes scanned the room, passing quickly over Adelaide and Noctus to settle on me and Astrid.

"I can hardly believe it," she gasped, pausing to raise a hand to her mouth.

"Thank you for agreeing to see us unannounced." I stood, as did Astrid, and that seemed to snap her out of her brief trance. "I would—"

The Queen of the Druids rushed forward, completely ignoring me, to gently cup Astrid's face with slender, trembling fingers.

"I nearly did not believe Raiden when he described our visitors. I feared I would never see you again, my dear Princess Elowen!"

Astrid

"What?" I croaked, staring at the queen in shock. Had she just called me a *princess?* And how did she know my real name?

Concern creased the beautiful queen's forehead. "Did your mother never tell you about her homeland?"

"She found it too painful to talk about her home and family," I said sadly. "But...how did you know her?"

The queen released my face, only to gently clasp my hands. "Forgive me, I forgot myself in my excitement. My name is Rowena Sylvaine, and I am your aunt."

I blinked. "I...never knew I had an aunt." My mother had never mentioned she had a sister. Did that mean I should be wary of her? Did she share her father's disdain for me?

Sorrow wilted the druid's delicate features, and her long ears drooped. "It saddens me to know she never spoke of me. But I suppose that was to be expected."

"Why? Were you one of those who chased her out?" The accusation came out harsher than I meant.

My aunt looked stricken. "No, of course not! I was the one who helped her escape with you that night!"

My lips parted in surprise. Jolene had mentioned my mother had received aid from another druid, one who had risked her own safety by doing so. "*You* were the one who helped her escape?"

Queen Rowena nodded gravely. "It sickened me to see what our father, King Orwen, did to your father. His obsession with the purity of our bloodline had always been a sore subject between us. But to defy him openly was to court banishment from the Druidlands. Had I not feared for my own husband and son, I would like to think I would have been braver."

Her voice trembled with emotion, so I gave her hands an encouraging squeeze. She smiled at me appreciatively.

"He dragged her back to Pyrcairn from where she had found happiness with her Harlandish soldier, and confined her to the deepest, darkest cell within the roots of our great tree. I visited her in secret as often as I could, and that was when I first held you, when you were but a wee thing. But my beloved older sister was wasting away from a broken heart in the darkness. Were it not for you, I think she may well have succumbed to her anguish. But *you* kept her going. And I knew that if I did nothing, I would lose the both of you forever."

"Was that when...?" I hated to imagine what my mother had gone through here.

She nodded. "I smuggled in a cloak and some food, put the guards to sleep, and helped her flee to the edge of the forest, near where I had seen the flying ships land. That was the last time I saw my sister and her daughter, until today." She stroked my cheek tenderly. "It was my greatest wish that she find happiness with you in a place where she could start over. When our father was killed by witches a few years ago, I began searching in earnest for you both, with little success. And yet here you are before me, having found your way home all on your own."

"How could you tell it was me?" My eyes misted at the love that radiated from her.

"You look so much like your mother. I could tell in a heartbeat it was you. But...why is she not with you? Is she well?" The earnest hope in her sparkling eyes made me reluctant to tell her the truth, but she deserved to know.

"My mother succumbed to the curse her father cast on her around the time I turned six." My lower lip trembled at the horror and grief on my aunt's face.

She drew me into a hug, gently stroking my back. "I am so sorry to hear that. I had no idea...we had hoped that the Astorians would know of a way to save her."

I nodded mutely, not trusting my voice.

After a moment, my aunt drew back, holding me at arm's length. She gave me a watery smile, and I could tell she was trying to be strong for my sake. "At least I will have the chance to get to know my darling little niece. Though I suppose you are not so little anymore."

I shook my head as my core throbbed with a painful reminder. How cruel was fate, that I should find family I never knew I had but not have much time to spend with her?

"No? Elowen, what is wrong?" The queen looked closer at me, her eyes flicking from my rounded ears to my blackened hair, and finally coming to rest near my heart. She gasped, a hand flying to her mouth, and shook her head in denial.

I nodded as tears dripped freely down my face, and with a shaky voice, admitted quietly, "The curse that killed my mother will soon take me as well."

Orion, who had remained silent through this whole exchange, suddenly lunged forward and roughly grabbed my arm, shaking me gently, ignoring the guard that stepped forward threateningly. "What do you mean, the curse will take you too?! What curse? And why am I only hearing about this now?!"

I shook my head, unable to form words around the lump in my throat. I had meant to keep this a secret until the end, but the kindness and the sympathy in the queen's eyes had somehow pulled it out of me.

"Is that why you have seemed so quiet lately?" Then his eyes widened with horror, and he touched the blackened tips of my hair before pushing up my sleeve to expose the darkened veins in my wrist. He worked his jaw for a moment. "*Why* did you not tell me?"

I looked away, but was met with Noctus' worried gaze instead. Orion released my wrist only to gently cup my face, forcing me to look at him.

"Why did you not ask me for help? For me to grant your wish?" he whispered hoarsely.

Would he still look at me the same if he knew the truth? Would the love shining so brightly in his eyes turn to hate? I felt a hysterical laugh try to bubble up my throat, but I swallowed it down. Was this what Orion had been thinking and feeling when he debated whether or not to reveal his true identity to *me?*

"I could never ask that of you," I rasped, shaking my head.

"Why in the name of the stars not?!" he cried.

I met his gorgeous blue eyes through a sheen of tears, fearing it was the last time he would look at me like this and engraving the sight on my corrupted heart.

"Because *I* am the reason you lost your mother."

Orion

I stared at Astrid in shock. Why would she blame herself for my mother's death? Unless... The puzzle pieces clicked into place. Why had I never thought of it before?

"You were the infant she used up her lifeforce to save."

Tears spilled from Astrid's reddened eyes as she looked down in shame, but she still nodded in confirmation. The queen watched me closely, a glint of both gratitude and resentment in her eyes.

I took a step back, releasing my hold on her. Confusion, hurt, and disbelief tore through me. *Why* had she never told me? Especially after I had bared my soul to her, after we had begun courting? But then I immediately felt like a hypocrite. It was not as if *I* had been forthcoming with the truth about myself either.

But then her earlier revelation struck me like a blow. "If my mother saved you from this—this curse your grandfather cast on you and your mother, then how is it still affecting you?"

"It was just...bad timing," Astrid explained hoarsely, shaking her head sadly. "Your mother had only just brought you into the world when my mother came begging her to save me. The curse was so powerful, so full of hatred, that an already-exhausted fallen star could barely manage to seal the curse, along with my magic, to keep it from progressing."

Her words rang true. I had already experienced first-hand how difficult it was to grant a wish when I was exhausted.

"But then what happened to the seal? Did it weaken over time?" I frowned. Astrid nearly always wore some sort of starsteel against her skin—that should have negated the effects of this curse, while at the same time boosting the magical seal my mother had created.

Astrid finally met my eyes. "The seal did grow weaker over time, but...I had to break the seal to use my magic. It was the only way."

"You broke it *on purpose?* Knowing what it would cost? Knowing what it would do to you?" I stared at her in numb disbelief. "By the stars, what was so important that you would throw it all away?" My voice cracked, and I resisted the urge to step forward and shake her shoulders. It felt like my heart was breaking all over again.

"You."

"What?"

"*You* were worth it. I was not throwing my life, your mother's gift and sacrifice, away! I was trading it for *yours!*" A spark of anger ignited in her voice as she gestured animatedly. "It was the *only* way to save you from Nyra's blade, and the only way to make an antidote strong enough to cure her magical poison."

I rocked back on my heels as the room went silent. Astrid had willingly doomed herself to save *me?* Even though I had been so foolishly and blindly in love with another? Love and gratitude warred with my shock, warmth filling my heart. I felt tears prick my eyes as the full meaning of what she had done hit me, stronger and more visceral than any of Rigel's blows.

What could I possibly say to her? To the person who had always stood by me, who had made the ultimate sacrifice without a second thought? How could I put into words the riotous emotions that were closing my throat and blurring my eyes?

"My father broke our most sacred taboo to cast that curse," Queen Rowena said sadly into the charged silence. "That terrible corruption of magic was forbidden long ago, after one depraved druid nearly destroyed every living creature in Sylvaine."

"Does that mean a solution was discovered to this curse?" Noctus asked quietly. I had nearly forgotten he was in the room, but hope soared in my chest at his question.

I had already lost my parents. I could not bear the thought of losing anyone else. Especially Astrid.

The queen looked troubled. "After my sister escaped, I spent years searching through our archives for a way to undo what my father had done. There is a way."

Astrid whirled towards her aunt, a painful hope shining in her eyes. "There is?"

"However...I am uncertain if it will be effective on you, my dear, as you are only half druid," she said gently. "And it would make changes in you, too."

"You speak of the Sacred Willow," Adelaide said quietly. Rafe crept slowly over to Astrid, pinning his ears when the queen shooed him away.

"Do not defile it with your putrid tongue, witch," the queen hissed, hatred darkening her fair visage. "Had Elowen not been with you, I would have had you beheaded on sight."

Noctus and Rafe moved a little closer to Adelaide protectively.

"Can this Sacred Willow save her or not?" I finally managed to ask. If the druids could undo what they had done, that would be best. But if the risk to Astrid was too much...

The special star-shaped pendant my mother had left for me weighed heavily on my chest. I had been saving it for the day I faced Nyra and her small army and routed them from my home. But I would use it in a heartbeat to save Astrid instead. What point would there be in retaking the kingdom if the castle remained empty of my friends?

"For generations, each Sylvaine prince or princess has communed with the Sacred Willow the night before they are crowned the next King or Queen. I, too, completed this ritual a few years ago, when I became Interim Queen until we could locate your mother. It is a sacred rite, when the ruler of the forest and all of its magic become one." Queen Rowena clasped Astrid's hands. "If you are willing to become our new Queen, then you may also undergo this ritual. The Sacred Willow will burn away any impurities in your magic and your body. But once you tie your soul to the forest, you will never be able to leave it again."

Orion

"Unless, of course...this self-proclaimed prince can grant your wish here and now," Queen Rowena drawled, her eyes narrowing on me.

Every eye turned on me, but I was still attempting to wrap my head around the fact that Astrid was a lost druid princess. But it was her eyes that cut me to the core. There was no hint of expectation in her eyes, as she already knew my answer before it left my lips.

"I hope to learn how—"

But before I could force the words out, Astrid jumped in. "My curse already cost him his mother, Aunt Rowena. I refuse to ask for the same sacrifice from *him*, when he has already saved my life several times over."

The queen scowled. "What difference does one more make? If he truly *is* the starborn prince, it should be a simple enough task." She turned to address me. "You came here seeking an alliance, did you not? What better way to prove your sincerity and win our loyalty than by saving our princess and your companion?"

I wanted to melt into the floor. "I had been originally hoping to strike a deal with the druids for a set number of wishes to be granted in the future—"

"In the *future?* This wish needs granting *now!* What sort of friend uses his so-called friend's life as a bargaining chip?" the queen demanded, drawing herself up to her full height. "If *this* is the sort of conduct we can expect from—"

"Believe me, Queen Rowena, if I knew how to grant her wish, I would have already done so!" I ground out, casting aside all etiquette I had been taught in the onslaught of her damning questions.

For a moment, the queen was too stunned to speak. After a minute, she stammered out, "But are you not the son of a fallen star? How could you not...?"

"As Astrid so *clearly* pointed out, my mother returned to the stars on the day of my birth. My father knew *only* how to use the amulet she left behind, but I lost both him *and* the amulet to the Woman-King when she betrayed me." I fought to keep my tone even, to keep my voice from catching on the lump that rose in my throat whenever I spoke of my father.

The queen's eyes softened a fraction, but I could not bear to meet Astrid's eyes just yet.

"I learned only recently that I inherited my mother's starpower, and therefore have yet to discover how to use it," I continued. Then I lifted the star pendant from beneath my shirt and let it dangle in front of me. "This is all that I have left of her now. It has the power to grant one wish. But I fear that, if the fallen star herself could not undo this curse, that her token would fail to do so as well. Nevertheless, I am willing to try—for Astrid's sake, and her sake alone."

I finally met her eyes, which were glimmering with emotion. She, more than anyone else here, understood what this meant to me. I withdrew the cord from around my neck. "This was crafted so that even those without starpower can make their wish."

The queen reached out to take it from me, but I moved it away. Before she could say anything about it, I stepped up to Astrid. I gently brushed aside her long hair so I could drape it around her neck.

"Please use it," I whispered hoarsely. If my mother's power could save her twice, I would be eternally grateful.

Astrid's fingers closed over the pendant, and to my surprise, she placed her other hand on my chest and kissed me in front of everybody. I speared my hand through her hair, and kissed her back with a tender ferocity. The thought of losing her too was unbearable to me.

The queen noisily cleared her throat, and we broke apart, but I did not shy away from meeting her gaze. "It seems I have much to discuss with my niece. If you would excuse us, I will have Raiden show you to the gardens."

I met Astrid's gaze, and at her tiny nod, accepted the queen's proposal. She ushered Astrid out of the room and down the moss-carpeted hall, and I heard a door close softly after they entered.

"Follow me," Raiden eventually said, eyeing me with blatant curiosity.

Noctus, Adelaide and Rafe took the lead, sensing that I needed some space to think. Birken fell in behind me, just as he had on the way here. We followed the druid down a series of twisting corridors for long enough that I started to lose my sense of direction. Suddenly, we emerged into the bright sunlight, with a magnificent garden spread out before us. I glanced back the way we had come, and saw that we had exited beside the huge tree.

The walled garden boasted beautiful flower beds with fountains interspersed throughout. Meandering stone paths wound through the lush greenery, and droves of butterflies and bees floated from flower to flower.

At a wave from me, Noctus, Adelaide and Rafe meandered further into the garden, though I doubted Noctus would go far. With a nod, Raiden went back into the tree, no doubt to guard the room where his queen now dwelled. But Birken stayed behind.

"For a prince with no kingdom, your arrogance knows no bounds," Birken sneered once Raiden was out of earshot. "The only reason you were permitted to enter was because of Princess Elowen. You have nothing more to offer us but trouble."

"At least *I* have the courage to do something about the problem facing both our countries," I snarled defensively. I was not in the mood to be mocked, no matter how true his accusations rang.

"What are you trying to say?" Birken brandished his spear, so I grabbed the hilt of my sword, readying to defend myself.

"Captain Beowin has called for you," Raiden said to Birken as he emerged from the shadowy entryway behind us.

Birken immediately withdrew his weapon, stiffening like a child caught breaking a rule he had been told specifically not to break. With another sneer at me, he turned and hurried back into the tunnel, looking pointedly ahead instead of at Raiden.

I released my hold on the hilt of my sword, eyeing Raiden with renewed interest. Had he waited in the shadows the whole time, knowing the other druid would be unable to resist taunting me?

"Apologies for Birken's behavior. Among the Queen's Riders, he is particularly antagonistic to outsiders." Raiden's apology surprised me.

"I certainly understand where he was coming from. He was not exactly wrong." I ran a hand through my hair, letting out a sigh of frustration.

I felt like a useless prince without a kingdom, just as Birken had said. Trouble seemed to follow me like a shadow, and I had little to offer the druids now—especially after I had just handed over the one wish I could still grant.

"Nonetheless, it was short-sighted of him to antagonize the starborn prince," Raiden commented.

The way he said *the starborn prince* tickled my memory, and I suddenly recalled that was the same phrase Astrid had used when she had seen me save Rigel's life.

"You speak as if my coming was foretold," I joked.

"It was."

My smile froze. "Excuse me?"

"Our previous king's father, King Redthorne, was imparted a prophecy from the Sacred Willow that most druids disregarded as the ramblings of an old druid."

"But...*you* believed him?" It dawned on me that Raiden was far older than he appeared.

He dipped his chin, and began to recite.

"When darkness descends from the mountainous land,

And our green forest is overrun by sand,

Then shall the starborn prince appear,

Aided by the witch and the druid to dispel all fear."

I stared at him. "And you believe *me* to be this starborn prince?"

"I have yet to encounter any other sons of fallen stars, who just so happen to be royalty and just so happen to be accompanied by a witch and a druid."

"The forest being overrun by sand clearly refers to the desert tribesmen," I mused, my mind whirling over the possibilities. "But what about this 'darkness'?"

"The witches. They fly here from their mountainous home on broomsticks to attack us frequently," Raiden supplied.

I sighed. "I do not suppose there are any additional lines to this prophecy pertaining to how, exactly, I can 'dispel all fear'?"

"No."

"Of course not. That would be far too practical and helpful," I grumbled. Then a new thought occurred to me. "Does Queen Rowena believe in this prophecy?" If she did, would she be more willing to aid my cause because of it?

But Raiden shook his head. "Our queen holds little faith in past kings. However, the fact that she has not ordered the execution of the witch who travels with you may mean she has not entirely disregarded it, either."

"I see." That was not the answer I had been hoping for, but at least it was not the one I had been fearing, either.

"There is a bench down that path, if you would like a quiet place to think, where you will not be disturbed," Raiden said, pointing at the pathway on the right. "I imagine it will be at least an hour before the queen calls for your party once more."

"Thank you for the recommendation...and the information." With a nod of thanks, I turned and meandered down the path he had indicated, smiling to myself at the slight rustling I heard nearby. Noctus had stayed close, but was considerate enough to give me space to think. He had always been quick to pick up on things like that.

After a few minutes of walking, I came across a wooden bench that sat beneath an archway which was covered in a flowering vine. I took a seat, watching the butterflies dancing between flowers as I attempted to sort through my tangled thoughts and emotions.

The truth about Astrid had taken us all by surprise—including her, apparently. Who would have guessed that Astrid—or Elowen, as they called her—was the daughter of the current queen's older sister? I chuckled drily at the thought that I was no longer the only one with two sets of names. But my smile died at the memory of her darkened hair and the bruise-like circles under her eyes. I wanted to kick myself for not realizing sooner. I had simply assumed she was exhausted, as we all were. I had not even considered the possibility of an illness, or a curse.

I still felt wounded that she had kept that from me, even if I understood the reason why. Astrid had always been too kind for her own good, and I had come so close to losing her because of it, without even knowing why. I had been oblivious to the weight of the guilt she carried, a guilt that did not belong to her. It had been my mother's decision to help her. She had known the risks.

Astrid must have feared the resentment against starpower that I had borne for so long, for taking my mother from me, would be turned on *her* if she told me the truth. Memories played in my mind's eye of Astrid cowering behind bars when the slaver captured us, of her proudly showing me her first successful remedy, of her laughing with joy as we raced across the rooftops under the light of the stars. I remembered the way her warm, brown eyes came alive when she was teaching Nova and Castor, and the way they had deepened into molten pools the first time I kissed her.

I could *never* blame her for the loss of my mother. If anything, it was a miracle we had found each other. She was the most precious gift my mother could have given me.

But to think that she had willingly chosen to sacrifice her life for mine... I put my head in my hands. What if the magic in that star pendant was not strong enough to save her?

"Are you...all right?" a voice asked hesitantly.

I looked up to see Adelaide fidgeting in front of me, Rafe by her side. I hesitated, then patted the bench beside me. Perhaps talking with her could help me figure out a way to save Astrid and this alliance. She sat down carefully, as if I were a deer she was trying not to startle.

"How do witches cast hexes?" I asked bluntly. "How do you access and channel your magic without a conduit?"

She looked surprised, then thoughtful. "My magic dwells in my core. To use it, I pull it towards my hands, and then guide it towards my target while envisioning what I want my magic to do. Unless I use special items to amplify my magic, whatever hex I cast is not permanent."

I mulled that over. "Is that why witches rarely attack from afar?" All of the reports I had read stated that witches could only attack you if you were within a specific range.

"Yes. Though with the proper materials, runes, and enough magic power, a witch can cast a powerful hex from afar. Just before I left my coven, the headwitch caused an earthquake in the Yellowboils' territory."

I blinked. "The three covens fight amongst themselves?"

"Frequently. There is a fierce rivalry among the covens." Rafe yawned, and Adelaide petted his head idly.

"Interesting." I steepled my fingers, mulling over what I had just learned.

Adelaide's description of how she cast hexes eerily echoed the process I had used to grant wishes using the amulet. When I had saved Rigel, I had used the depleted amulet as a guide. But what if the key was simply doing the exact same thing, except by drawing the magic from my own core, instead of the reservoir within the amulet?

"How about you try to locate and access your core? Rafe and I will keep watch." The witch smiled at me reassuringly, and I nodded in agreement.

I closed my eyes in concentration, trying to sense that elusive well of magic like I had earlier. I dove deep inside myself, following the faint path of glimmering starlight. I smiled in triumph when I found it, determined to memorize what it had felt like to do so. Now, I just needed to call it forth.

I tried pulling at it, like Adelaide had described, but the shimmering ball of starlight hardly flickered. Was I trying to call too much of it at once? I visualized a thin stream of magic, flowing from my core, up my arms, and to my hands, the way I would guide the amulet's magic.

At first, nothing happened. But then, like a stream beginning to flow down a mountain from its icy source, a thin line of starlight began to trickle towards my hands.

"I think you are doing it!" I heard Adelaide murmur excitedly as she inched closer and closer.

I felt a spark of foreign magic as her hand closed over mine in a vise-like grip. My eyes flew open with alarm, my concentration shattered. And that was when I heard the screams.

"Attack! The witches are attacking!"

Astrid

"**I** can still hardly believe you are here." The queen had refused to relinquish my hand since we sat down in another naturally-upholstered room, just down the hall from the first one.

"I can hardly believe it myself." I could clearly see her resemblance to my mother; they both had the same high cheekbones, delicate chin, and arched brows. Had my mother's hair and eyes not been darkened by the curse, they would have been nearly identical.

"How did my sister spend her final years? Was she able to find some measure of peace and happiness?"

"I believe so." I smiled as I recalled what memories I could of my mother. "She worked in an apothecary's shop to support us, and every rest day, she would take me to the market to try a new sweet treat."

"I am relieved to hear that," my aunt murmured, her eyes turning bright.

"She was incredibly strong. She never took off her starsteel jewelry, but even with that special metal and her abstinence from using her magic, I could tell she was often pained by headaches, or became short of breath. She tried to hide it from me, but eventually was forced to tell me the truth, and the reason why I was never allowed to touch the sparkles inside of me."

"And she never petitioned the king for a wish?" There was an edge of anger in her voice that I knew was caused by her grief.

"Of course not. She had used her wish to save my life, and knew the widower king would have turned her away at the door. Though I do not believe he blamed her for the loss of his wife, he would have never risked leaving his newborn son orphaned."

The queen paused, and I could see how she struggled to contain her grief. I set my hand on top of hers, and she smiled at me gratefully.

"It was wise of you to seek out the prince," she eventually commented.

I shook my head in denial. *"He* was the one who found *me.* Were it not for him, I would have been sold as a slave, doomed to toil in Harland's salt mines for the rest of my life."

I went on to explain how the boy who called himself Orion had come to my rescue, shortly after my mother had passed, when Khalifon had captured me and dozens of other children off the streets. I told her about how he had placed me in Evelyn's

Home for Children, and about how I had become an herbalist and joined his guild to help him save others.

"You truly had no idea he was Prince Sterling?" My aunt's lips thinned as she listened to all I had been through.

"Not until recently. Since I had never used my own magic, I was unable to sense his. But the first time I saw him grant a wish, I knew he was the starborn prince from the rhyme my mother had taught me."

"That *rhyme* is a prophecy that has been passed down in our family since the days of my grandfather. I never expected it to come true in my lifetime, though I should have guessed when the fallen star fell in love with a human." She drummed her fingers against the wooden table contemplatively.

"Would the druids—would you—ally with him? To drive back the tribesmen?" I asked hopefully, belatedly remembering why we had come in the first place.

"My only wish was to find my sister and her daughter, a wish he has inadvertently granted by bringing you here. We will not ally with a kingdomless royal, even if he *is* the starborn prince of prophecy. I absolutely refuse to lose any more loved ones to a war not of my making." Her tone was firm, though her eyes begged me to understand.

"Have you not already lost some to the tribesmen crossing through Sylvaine on their way to Astoria?"

The queen went quiet, so I knew the answer to my question. "We are a small queendom. We cannot afford to become involved in a conflict that seems sure to burn half the continent to the ground, should the tribesmen attack in earnest."

"Do you truly believe the Woman-King will be satisfied with *just* taking Astoria? When the Druidlands are even richer in natural resources than the kingdom of the stars?" I asked quietly.

"Either way, *you* will not be around to see it unless you undergo the ritual to become our next queen," she said gently, not-so-subtly changing the subject.

My fingers found the star-shaped pendant Orion had given me, my first glimmer of hope in this darkness. "Or I could use this."

"You heard the boy—if even the magic of a *true* fallen star could not dispel the curse, then it is doubtful this mere trinket could. And you cannot afford to wait for him to learn to wield his own magic properly," my aunt rebutted.

I bit my lip. "But what if I refuse—"

Suddenly, the queen went deathly still, her fair skin paling even further. Her long, pointed ears twitched this way and that, but no matter how much I strained, I could hear no cause for alarm.

"Pyrcairn is under attack—it must be the witches!" She stood, hauling me up with her. She pinned me with a look. "That witch you brought must have led them right to us!"

My eyes widened. "Adelaide would never! She cut off all contact with her coven many months ago."

"And how would you know if she truly did, if neither you nor the princeling can sense her magic properly?" she hissed.

I thought quickly. "Then let us find her, and see for ourselves if she will fight with us to defend Pyrcairn. And I will fight with you!"

I reached for my bow, intending to find Orion and the others and help defend this hidden sanctuary. I gritted my teeth as a wave of sudden dizziness washed through me, cursing the corruption in my magic and its impeccable timing.

"No!" Queen Rowena cried, her blue eyes widening in alarm. She snatched my bow away. "I forbid it! I refuse to lose you again, after having only just found you. You will stay here, where it is safest, until I return for you. And *this,* young one, is what comes of trusting a witch."

Before I could argue, she swept out of the room, the carved wooden doors magically closing and locking behind her. I grabbed the door handle and tried to turn it, but it was stuck fast. I wildly looked around, searching for another way out. My eyes fell on the window opposite the door, which was more of a cut out than a true window with glass.

I experimentally moved my hand through the opening, and felt relieved to discover there was no magical barrier there. My aunt must have forgotten about it in her haste to join the battle.

After checking to make sure none of the frantic druids I could see were looking towards the window, I carefully climbed out of it. The hem of my ridiculous dress snagged on the unpolished wood, so I yanked on it until it tore free.

I heard a loud *boom,* followed by a tremor beneath my feet from the impact. What kind of hexes were the witches casting?! And where had Orion and the others been taken? I scanned my surroundings frantically as I began to run. My eyes swept over court druids and soldiers alike taking up arms. Most were heading to the west, where the bulk of the noise was coming from.

I started heading that way as well. If I knew Orion, he would join the fight without a second thought. Which meant he would need someone to watch his back.

As I was passing what looked to be an ornate garden, I heard ferocious barking coming from within it. Rafe! I veered down a stone pathway and followed the sound. After a few twists and turns, I found Orion and Adelaide standing by a bench, a strange look on Orion's face. Noctus appeared from the shadowy foliage to my right, and I was relieved to see none of them had been harmed.

"Tell me you had nothing to do with this," Orion asked Adelaide, his hand drifting towards the hilt of his sword.

The witch shook her head vehemently. "I swear by the stars I had no hand in this! If I had, I would have slipped away to join them when the druids brought us to this secluded garden."

"Then what was the magic I felt from you just now, when you grabbed my hand?" Orion's eyes narrowed.

Adelaide paused. "When you were trying to connect with your magic just now, you did not seem to hear me. I was trying to snap you out of your trance before the battle reached us."

After a moment, Orion nodded, seeming to accept this explanation. But I glanced between the two, a feeling of unease twining around my heart. But now was not the time for that.

"This might be your best opportunity to leave, while the queen is distracted," I broke in.

Orion's smile at my reappearance faltered. *"Leave?* While our potential allies are under attack?"

"Queen Rowena has no intention of allying with you, even if she has not completely disregarded the prophecy. And if she believes that Adelaide led those witches here...well, it would be better to escape now." I looked at Adelaide and Rafe solemnly.

Orion cursed, running a hand through his hair. "Do you think our aid in this fight against the witches could convince her otherwise?"

"It is difficult to say," I said slowly. I had not exactly known her long enough to predict what she would do.

A fireball whistled over our heads before it smashed into the tree-building behind us with a resounding *boom.* We all flinched, and Rafe hunched to the ground, his tail tucked between his legs and an anxious whine coming from his throat.

"Rafe was originally captured by witches, likely during a raid similar to this," Adelaide explained softly when we looked at her questioningly. "As far as I can tell, he hates all other witches on principle."

There was a strangled cry above us as a witch on a broomstick was struck by a druid's arrow and came crashing down to the ground. She skidded to a stop not far from us, blood trickling from her chapped and twisted lips. She wore tattered rags, and her tanned and wrinkled skin sported a horrifying number of angry-looking boils.

I reached for my bow as her beady eyes narrowed on us and she gave me a gap-toothed grin. I cursed when my hand found only empty air. Orion drew his sword and darted forward, swiftly parting her head from her body before the malevolent magic swirling around her could coalesce into a hex. I glanced at Adelaide, relieved to see that she seemed entirely unperturbed by the scene.

"This is a witch from the Yellowboil Coven," she announced, frowning. "But why would the southernmost coven come so far northeast?"

"Is that unusual?" I asked.

"They would have risked the wrath of the Blackleach Coven by trespassing on their territory and violating the non-aggression pact," Adelaide answered. "Unless they flew over only Harland..."

Noctus shook his head. "If an entire coven had flown over Harland, we would have heard about it. Can a hex cause the illusion of invisibility?"

"Not over so many at once."

Orion paled. "The witches are not the only ones adept at illusion magic."

"Do you suspect...?" I trailed off, putting a hand to my mouth.

"I would not exactly put it past Nyra to strike a deal with a coven to get what she wants," he growled. "She claimed to have refused to offer her people as sacrifices before. Could she have changed her mind? Or was that another one of her lies?"

Another fireball whistled overhead, a pair of witches following behind it with looks of concentration and glee on their pocked faces. Rafe pinned his ears back.

"Noctus, I want you with me. Adelaide, Rafe, protect Astrid and support us from behind. We are going to take down as many of these witches as we can," Orion ordered as he drew his starsword.

"But—" I protested.

"Even if we tried to escape amid the chaos, we would be lost in the magical barriers that protect this forest. Besides, we are not leaving here until your curse is broken—one way, or another." Orion pinned me with his icy blue stare, and I could tell by the set of his jaw that there would be no talking him out of it.

"Fine."

"Here, I brought a spare." Noctus tossed me a bow from the motley assortment of weapons he kept with him at all times.

"I know I can always count on you." I smiled at him gratefully as I nocked an arrow to the taut bowstring. I felt much better with a weapon in my hands.

With Orion leading the way, we charged out of the garden and into the fray.

Orion

I dodged one fireball and cut another in half with my sword as I entered the battle, the starsteel negating the magic so that the deadly fireball evaporated in a puff of smoke. After what that scratch from Nyra had done to me, I was extra careful not to let anything so much as graze me.

Witches were swarming everywhere, on the ground and in the sky. Young druid children ran screaming from the malicious invaders, doing everything they could to avoid being hexed. Those who could fight bound their opponents with nearby vines or fought them with spears.

Many of the druids' quaint homes were burning, the smoke filling the air with a gray haze that stung my eyes and burned the back of my throat. Injured elk, wild with pain from their wounds, bolted through the fray, heedless of whether they trampled friend or foe beneath their massive hooves.

A group of mounted druid warriors charged at a quartet of powerful witches, their long spears lowered. One druid threw his spear like a javelin, piercing one witch, but cried out in horror when he and his mount were turned to ice by another witch.

The witch in the lead cackled as she pointed her crooked finger at a druid's mount, and he fell onto his face as his massive elk shrank into a tiny mouse. Another druid wrapped that witch in a spiky cocoon of thorny vines, and squeezed it smaller, until the figure inside ceased struggling.

The remaining druids scattered to dodge a massive fireball, which exploded against a bakery in a fiery cyclone. The druid, whose mount had been shrunk, rose unsteadily to his feet, only to have feathers sprout from his skin as he was turned into a sparrow.

As the two remaining witches prepared to end the other druids, Astrid's arrow thunked into the chest of one witch, while the second was enveloped by Adelaide's reddish magic, and rapidly shrank into the form of a rat. Rafe made short work of the rat.

I saw a witch flying towards a druid's unprotected back as he fought off another witch atop his elk. "Astrid!" I called, and within moments, the witch fell from the sky, an arrow in her chest. Before she could try to cast one last hex, I swiftly ended her. Noctus brought down a third witch.

After dispatching his own opponent, the druid turned, but stopped short when he saw me standing over the witch's body.

"What are you four doing out here?" Birken's usual sneer had been replaced by the grim set of his mouth.

Rafe barked at him, seemingly offended to be excluded from the count. Birken rolled his eyes, but made no effort to correct himself.

"Saving you, it would seem." I scanned the battlefield as I spoke, my gaze passing over those who looked like they could handle themselves. "Where are reinforcements needed the most?"

Birken pointed with his spear. "There, at the entrance to the Queen's Palace. I suspect they may be targeting her."

"Understood. I will leave this area to you." Without waiting for a response, I gestured to the others and led the way deeper into the carnage.

"Adelaide, can you cast a glamour on all of us, to make us look like witches, but only to other witches?" I asked.

"Only if you are not touching any starsteel." Red magic began to gather around her.

"Just on Noctus and I then. If you can, please create a shield around Astrid," I said as I ripped a strip of cloth from the hem of my tunic and wrapped it around my sword hand.

Without my mother's necklace, I was keenly aware that I had no other starsteel on my body. I would be far more vulnerable to hexes than I ever had been before, right when I needed that protection the most. But if the enemy never saw me coming, it might just work out. After all, in the heat of battle, neither the druids nor the witches would have the time to pay attention to sensing what kind of magic I carried.

I approached a druid and a witch who were hurling magic at each other, and was thrilled when the witch hardly blinked at my approach.

"You there, cast a paralyzing hex on her!" the witch barked.

In lieu of a reply, I thrust my blade through her black heart. Her expression changed from one of glee to one of shock. I withdrew the starsword and wiped it clean as Astrid swiftly bandaged a nasty burn the druid had sustained.

Once she was taken care of, we wove through smoldering houses and storefronts on our way to the main entrance of the Queen's Palace, where we had also initially entered. I peeked around a corner and then held up my fist, the others stopping behind me.

The two grand doors had been shattered by a mighty hex, and fallen witches and druids lay scattered on the ground in front of them. Based on the trampled carpet of moss in the entryway, a large number of witches had already made it inside.

I ground my teeth. This attack felt all too similar to the way the tribesmen had taken my own castle. The fact that this building alone was not burning also gave credence to Birken's theory that they were looking for someone.

Astrid gasped when she cautiously looked around the corner as well, a hand flying to her mouth. "What if their goal is to kill my aunt?!"

"We will not let them," I told her firmly.

After scanning the area two more times, we ventured into the eerily quiet clearing. Noctus brought up the rear, walking backwards to ensure we were not taken by surprise. Rafe guarded our sides, his hackles raised and teeth bared menacingly.

I brought my guard up as a dozen witches came running and stumbling out of the entrance, many looking back over their shoulders fearfully. *What scared a witch?*

"Begone from this place!"

Queen Rowena strode out of the ruined doorway, her hands raised at her sides and glowing with magic. Everything around her responded to her call, and even the broken doors turned into deadly wooden spears that launched themselves at the witches, impaling two before they could throw up a protective barrier.

"We can catch them in a pincer attack. Noctus, take point with me," I instructed as I quickly analyzed the situation. Rafe barked before racing into the midst of the witches, making gleeful noises as he tore into the unsuspecting women. Clearly, the animal could hold a grudge.

The girls fell back, a combination of arrows and magical projectiles raining over our heads and into the ranks of the witches. Two more fell, the others turning in alarm just in time to see Noctus and I charging into their midst, blades drawn. I had discovered quite quickly that witches had no close-combat abilities; they were cowards who liked to strike from a safe distance. Their hexes took too long to conjure—our starsteel blades were far faster.

I cut down a witch as Noctus ended another. I glanced around for my next target, but had to dodge a fireball, and then another. The second wound up hitting the witch behind me, who went down with a shriek and a puff of smoke. Thanks to Astrid and Adelaide, now only half of our adversaries were still standing.

I had drifted closer to the queen, who was busy battling a pair of witches that took turns launching hexes at her. My gaze snagged on the sudden movements of the third witch crouching behind them, icicle spears forming in the air around her, as she aimed at the unsuspecting queen.

Thinking fast, I grabbed a wide shield from a fallen druid and sprinted towards the queen.

"Get behind me!" I yelled, bringing the heavy wooden shield up in front of us both mere moments before I felt the jarring impact of the spear-like icicles. My arm went numb, so I dropped the shield and switched my sword to my other hand. I had always grumbled about running drills with my weaker arm, but now I was immensely grateful for those grueling sessions with Sir Magnus and Sir Rigel.

"Thank you." The queen dipped her chin in reluctant acknowledgement.

"Anytime," I panted, grinning cheekily at her.

She raised her glowing hands, and the trees in the area came alive, their branches forming into massive clubs and their roots snaking onto the battlefield like living ropes to trip and bind the panicking witches.

Queen Rowena was incredibly powerful, and would make an even greater ally than I had imagined. I would have to think of something else to offer, to help convince her to join me. She was a force of nature, a force to be reckoned with.

"Remind me to never make you mad," I said with a relieved laugh as I watched the queen's small army of trees incapacitate the rest of the witches within moments.

She snorted, a very unladylike sound. "The sentiment is mutual."

With no more threats in sight, I sheathed my sword and worked on rubbing the feeling back into my right arm. Adelaide and Astrid approached sheepishly, and I realized why Astrid was acting strangely when the queen's eyes flew wide.

"I told you to remain in that room to keep you safe! How did you escape?!" she exclaimed, worry creasing her smooth brow.

"You imprisoned her?!" Alarmed, I moved to stand between the queen and Astrid, who put a hand on my arm.

"Only to keep her safe!" she retorted, her eyes never leaving Astrid.

"I am no stranger to fighting, and I refuse to cower in a corner when I could be making a difference out here!" Astrid retorted hotly.

Before the queen could retort, a muffled explosion sounded in the distance. A second followed the first, but from a different direction. The ground beneath our feet trembled and bucked, as if it were crying out in pain.

Queen Rowena's face went pale. "They must be trying to breach the Sacred Willow."

"Then we must stop them," Astrid asserted in a tone that brooked no room for argument.

"We will split up. Noctus, please aid the queen. Astrid, Rafe, Adelaide and I will go around the other side, so we can catch them between us in another pincer attack." I looked at each person in turn, waiting for a nod of confirmation from each of them.

"Elowen, please...be careful," the queen said softly to her niece. Her gaze hardened when it found mine. "Keep her safe."

"On my life," I swore solemnly.

Our group split into two, and we raced in opposite directions through the smoke, arrowing straight for the danger that threatened the heart of Pyrcairn.

Astrid

"Rafe, lead us to the witches who just caused those explosions!" Adelaide requested, and the wolf began trotting in front of us, his nose to the ground and his tail waving like a flag.

We followed him around a corner, and ran straight into another skirmish. Orion charged straight in, as did Rafe, and I laid down some cover, my arrows keeping any sneak-attackers at bay. Adelaide helped as well, and I was relieved to see that she seemed to have no qualms about taking out members of a rival coven. I still had to wonder whether she could do the same against those of her former coven.

I hoped I never had to find out.

"Thank you for your aid," panted one of the druids. Her long blonde hair was braided back into a ponytail, and a fierce passion burned in her clear eyes despite the wounds on her arms and legs. Similar injuries marred the other two druids who were slumped on the ground behind her. "I am called Ivy."

"Anytime, Ivy" Orion answered. "Did you see a large group of witches pass through here?"

"Yes—they breached the Queen's Palace. We tried to stop them, so they left those three witches behind to engage us while the rest went on ahead," Ivy reported, gesturing to the now fallen adversaries. I noticed she was eyeing Adelaide warily, but refrained from commenting.

"Those explosions must have been how they broke down the doors." I could see scorch marks around a large gap in the outer wall ahead of us.

"Correct." Ivy winced, putting a hand over a gash in her arm.

"Here." I pulled out a tincture and some gauze from my satchel and handed it to her. "Put this on your wounds and on your companions'. It will speed up the healing process."

"Thank you for your kindness, princess." She took the supplies and immediately got to work, tending to the worst of the other druids' injuries.

I flinched at the title, but fortunately, she did not seem to notice. I could still hardly believe my mother had failed to mention such an important detail to me. I could only guess that she hid the truth to prevent me from seeking out the druids in the hopes of an easier life, the kind most little girls always dreamed of having.

"We will go on ahead. Please send any fighting-fit druids you see after us." Orion nodded to Ivy before continuing on.

He paused a moment at the entrance, checking to make sure no witches were lying in wait.

"Wait," Adelaide said, stopping him before he could go inside. "Let me go first, so I can check for any traps."

Orion paused. "I did not think about that. Please, if you would." He gestured for her to take the lead, so she did, holding one glowing hand out before her, with Rafe right beside her.

She only made it a few steps before she paused, and her magic spread over a patch of the ceiling. I looked directly beneath it, and saw a druid slumped on the ground with a crude spear in his chest, his lifeless eyes still wide with shock.

"It certainly pays to have a witch on our side," I murmured to Orion. He nodded solemnly.

Once the trap had been disabled, I said a quick blessing over the body and gently closed his eyes. I was starting to understand why Queen Rowena and the other druids had been so hostile towards Adelaide since we arrived.

The witches' attacks truly were brutal and barbaric.

Adelaide paused several more times as we moved down the simple, but elegant hallways to disarm more traps. The path the witches had taken was easy to follow; they had left a trail of destruction in their wake. Fortunately, it seemed those who had chased after the coven before us had wised up to their tricks, since we found no more fallen druids after the first one.

Soon, however, we came to a circular room that had a total of six different pathways branching off it, including the one through which we had entered. We walked cautiously into the center of the room once Adelaide had cleared the one trap it contained.

"We must be close to the Sacred Willow," I commented. "I am not surprised the druids would try to confuse the uninitiated like this."

"Any idea which way we should go?" Orion asked.

I walked to the entrance of one of the paths, listening intently. Nothing. Adelaide and Orion mirrored my movements. I walked to the next one, and I could detect the sounds of fighting echoing through the passageway.

"This way!" I said, then paused as a wave of dizziness washed over me. No, not now!

"I hear fighting coming from this tunnel as well," Adelaide said, pointing to the leftmost passage. "Should we split up?"

Orion hesitated, then shook his head. "It would be better to stay together. Astrid?" he asked in alarm as I staggered. "Are you hurt?"

My knees gave out, and I felt a magical wind slow my fall long enough for Orion to catch me. I clutched at my heart, trying to pull in some air through the pain. It felt like a thousand knives were stabbing my lungs, forcing me to take only quick, shallow breaths. Darkness licked at the edges of my vision, but I fought it back.

"Astrid? Astrid! Can you hear me? Answer me!" I heard his voice as if from a great distance, his trembling fingers stroking my hair.

"Curse," I croaked out, before I had to grit my teeth against a new wave of agony. The attacks were getting worse.

"Where does she keep her pouch of stardust?" Adelaide cut in. "You need to feed some to her, perhaps sprinkle some more on her skin!"

The pain overwhelmed my senses, and the next thing I knew, Orion's lips were on mine, and stardust was tickling my tongue. I swallowed, and after a moment, the pain receded enough for me to think again. I blinked open my eyes to see a worried Orion and Adelaide hovering over me. I took a deep, shaky breath, and gave them a watery smile.

"Thanks."

"Have some more stardust, just in case." Orion held me close as he helped me eat a little more of the precious powder, and I closed my eyes in relief as the lingering sense of dizziness receded.

"I feel much better now." I felt safe in Orion's arms, and I almost wished we could simply stay like that forever.

But the echoes of the fierce battles being fought up ahead reminded me of what we had to do.

"You two—I mean, three," I amended when Rafe whined at me, "should keep going. I would only slow you down."

"I refuse to leave you behind," Orion said heatedly. "Besides, I promised the queen I would keep you safe."

"You also promised to help her eradicate these attackers," I reminded him. Still he hesitated. "Set me down over there. Once I catch my breath, I will follow you."

"I will *not* leave you unprotected." Orion had that stubborn set to his shoulders I had seen so many times before.

The wolf put his paw on my knee and looked up at Adelaide.

"Rafe wants to stay back with Astrid, to keep her safe." The witch turned her gaze on Orion. "And you and I can each take a tunnel. So long as your skin is touching your starsteel sword, most hexes should not work on you."

Still Orion hesitated, glancing at me. "Are you sure?"

"Go on—I will follow behind once I have caught my breath." I smiled at them both reassuringly, and rested a hand on Rafe's back.

He knelt down in front of me, and said sternly to Rafe, "Protect her for me." The wolf nodded. Then he pressed a light kiss to my forehead, soft as the rain. "Though darkness falls..."

I smiled, my heart warming at the comforting catchphrase. "Still the stars find their way."

After sharing a look with Adelaide, both of them turned and entered the two different passageways, their running footsteps quickly fading. I tried not to worry too much, knowing both of them were more than capable of taking care of themselves. Without me slowing them down, or distracting them, they could help the druids protect their home.

The sharp pains from earlier had receded into a dull ache, so I focused on breathing in deeply through my nose and out through my mouth, the way my mother had taught me. I dimly wondered what she would have thought of the bizarre situation I found myself in. Would she have been happy I reconnected with her sister, and that her abuser was gone? Or would she be disappointed that I broke my promise to her and returned to her homeland against her wishes?

The sounds of battle grew fiercer, and then quieted down. I hoped that meant my friends had succeeded in defeating the witches. Rafe licked my face, and I giggled.

"Thank you for staying with me. Despite what I told the others, I think I would have been anxious if I were alone." I scratched the wolf behind the ears, and he gave me a wolfish grin, his tongue lolling out like a dog's.

Suddenly, his ears flicked back towards the tunnel Adelaide had taken, and he whipped his head around, cocking it to the side as he listened intently. He stood and raced over to the mouth of the passage, then looked back and barked at me.

My heart sped up. "Is Adelaide in danger?"

Rafe barked again, took a few steps forward, then paused to look at me. He clearly wanted me to follow him.

"Then we need to help her." I struggled to my feet, using the wall for support, and slung my borrowed bow over my shoulder.

I stumbled over to Rafe, my steps gaining more confidence by the time I reached him. He let me rest my hand on his back, and pulled me deeper into the passage. The longer we walked, the more damage we saw. Scorch marks and slashes from spears marred the wooden walls, and before long, we began to pass by the still figures of witches and druids alike.

We came upon a number of spots where the passage would split into two or even three different branches, but Rafe never hesitated. Embers glowed where hexes had exploded, telling me we were fast approaching what remained of the fighting.

I could see a strange, bluish-white light at the end of the tunnel, which was littered with fallen fighters. We approached cautiously, and exited the passage into a cavernous room. It was circular, and the walls were grooved wood, as if we were inside the very center of the great tree's trunk. Unlike the rest of the rooms and passages, there were no decorations or adornments. And at the very center of the room stood the most beautiful willow tree I had ever seen.

The trunk was a pale beige, but at its base it split in two. The gap between the twin trunks glowed with a ferociously powerful amount of magic. It was the same magic I had sensed in the other druids, except in its purest, rawest form. All of its leaves also glowed a bluish-white, but they paled in comparison to the magic between the trunks.

Dimly glowing flowers surrounded the base of the trunk, and a pond lay in a wide moat around it. The water was so still that its surface acted as a silvery mirror.

Was this the Sacred Willow my aunt had spoken of? The one that could save me only by chaining me here?

A number of fallen witches and druids littered the ground between my passage and the willow, but I saw no movement. Surely not all of the druids had been defeated alongside the witches, right? And where was Adelaide?

Rafe pricked his ears forward, a second before I heard the sound of voices. I pulled us down behind a couple of still witches, counting on the shadows to hide us at this distance so long as we held still. Two people walked around the willow, but I could not distinguish who they were. They were silhouetted against the bright magic of the tree. I strained to hear what they were saying as they slowly drew closer.

"Now that all of those disgusting Yellowboils are out of the picture, I want a full report of your mission," crooned one of the two. Based on her stooped figure and the rasp in her voice, I guessed her to be a witch.

"Of course, Headwitch Brunhilde."

I stifled a gasp. That was Adelaide's voice! My grip tightened on Rafe's fur, and I looked over to see that he had raised his hackles. If Adelaide was calling her *headwitch*, did that mean that hag was the leader of the Redgrave Coven?!

"After infiltrating Astoria, I located the source of that strong magical power. It belonged to the son of the last known fallen star, the fugitive Prince Sterling Astoria. I successfully gained the trust of the prince and most of his companions, and was just about to capture him when the Yellowboils attacked," Adelaide reported in a meek tone I had rarely heard from her before.

I could not believe my ears. A strange numbness buzzed in my fingertips. Adelaide was *still* a Redgrave? She had been lying to me since the moment we met!

"Excellent," Headwitch Brunhilde cackled. "And this fool still trusts you?"

"Yes, Headwitch." After a brief pause, she asked tentatively, "And if I may be so bold, may I ask why you are personally assisting the Yellowboils?"

"I will allow it. The Woman-King proposed a deal to all three covens; whichever coven could locate the prince first could keep him and his powers, after she was done with him, so long as he never set foot outside of the Varlett Witchlands again."

I sucked in a quiet breath. I could hardly believe what I was hearing. Nyra had put a bounty on his head?! So that was how she planned to get rid of the threat he posed—by having the witches do the dirty work for her!

Adelaide gasped. "All of the covens know about him now?!"

"Are there spiders in your ears? I just told you they do!" Brunhilde snarled. Adelaide wilted. Rafe tensed. "Which is why we must capture him first. I would sooner hex myself than see another coven take the fallen star's offspring!"

"He is near—in these very tunnels," Adelaide said excitedly. "If I am the one to bring him to you, will you release my final seal?" There was a hint of desperation in her voice.

"I will abide by our original bargain. No prince, no powers." The old hag cackled.

The memories of all the time I had spent with Adelaide flashed through my mind. None of it had been real. She had always been using me to get to Orion. She must have approached me that day knowing who I was, getting into my good graces only so I would lead her to him.

A sneer twisted my lips. She was no better than Khalifon. She and Nyra could have been twins. And I felt like the biggest fool of all for trusting her. Once again, I had brought danger to the one person I wanted so badly to protect.

Adelaide had betrayed us all.

I had to tell the others. I had to warn Orion! He and my aunt were walking straight into a trap!

Hardly daring to breathe, I began to inch backwards in a crouch. I could follow the trail of destruction back to that circular room and take the branch that Orion had gone down. Hopefully, that passage did not lead here as well. But I needed to hurry, just in case.

And that was when Rafe whined.

The witches' head whipped in our direction, and crimson eyes found mine.

Orion

"Watch out!" I shoved the queen aside, so I could cleave the malevolent ball of magic in half.

Before the witch who had cast it could react, Queen Rowena had bound and gagged the warty hag with vines that had appeared at her feet. The witch struggled, but I let out a sigh of relief. That had been the final witch in this passageway. The rest of her kind all lay either utterly defeated or bound and gagged with vines, ropes, or even tree branches.

Thanks to our sudden appearance, the druids who had been on the verge of defeat had rallied. While there had still been casualties, a good dozen of them stood strong behind me. They were worn, but still very much able to continue fighting.

"That was the last of them in this area," Noctus reported. He and a druid sentry had scouted to make sure none of the attackers were hiding or had slipped away from us in the chaos of battle.

"Good job. Have any of the witches talked?"

Noctus shook his head. "They are fanatically devoted to their headwitch. Not one is willing to reveal their mission here."

"Did you apply starsteel?"

Noctus blinked. "That did not occur to me."

"Perhaps being disconnected from their powers might loosen a few tongues," I said grimly.

"Marvelous idea." The queen strode over to her captive, and secured starsteel manacles around her wrists. She then commanded the vine gagging her to loosen. "What is your objective? And how did you find this place?"

The witch sneered at her. "You will find out soon enough."

"I wonder what would happen if I inserted slivers of starsteel into your wounds, and then kindly stitched them up for you," the queen drawled, a ruthless slant to her eyes.

The witch's eyes widened a fraction before darting this way and that. I had to remind myself that Astrid's aunt was a queen, one who had lost her husband and son to the same enemy that now threatened her niece and the rest of those under her care.

"Even if you torture and kill me now, you are already too late!" Beads of sweat stood out on her wrinkled forehead. She wriggled, as if trying to free herself from her bonds.

The queen scowled. "Your headwitch is already my prisoner. If you answer my questions, you may not have to share in her fate."

The witch bared her crooked yellow teeth. Several were missing. "My headwitch would never allow herself to be captured by a sniveling druid, not when there is such a great prize to be won!"

Prize? What prize? Unease shivered down my spine.

"Noctus, go check on Astrid." To the queen, I asked, "What lies at the end of the leftmost passage that branches off from the circular room?"

The queen paled. "Why do you ask?'

"Is it the Sacred Willow?" I watched the witch carefully, and saw the slightest reaction to my words. The queen saw it too.

"This was just a diversion!" She looked near panicked. If the witches tampered with it, would it no longer be able to cure Astrid?

"Astrid is gone," Noctus panted as he sprinted up to me. I had never seen him look so distraught, except for when he had told me how those tribesmen had hurt her last time. "And I did not pass her in the tunnels, so she must have followed Adelaide."

"Unless more witches came through behind us," I said grimly.

"Half of you stay here to guard the prisoners. Everyone else, with me!" the queen called, her lips pursed in a worried line.

I sheathed my sword and led the way back through the passages, retracing my steps from earlier. Sure enough, when I arrived in the large circular room of branching paths where I had left Astrid, she was nowhere to be seen.

Without stopping, I dove into the tunnel Adelaide had taken, the numerous scorch marks and fallen witches assuring me I was on the right path. After a few more twists and turns, I could see a strange light emanating from the end of the tunnel. Had I taken a wrong turn somewhere?

"I can scarcely believe you left her alone with the witch!" the queen hissed angrily.

"Adelaide and Rafe have protected her before. Without them, you might have never gotten to see Astrid again," I said tightly.

Despite my words, I fought back my sense of rising panic. What if another group of witches really *had* come through? What if Adelaide had been overcome by sheer numbers?

If worse came to worse, at least Astrid still had my star pendant.

We ran towards the light, the pattering of footsteps echoing behind us. The mouth of the tunnel must have been where the fiercest fighting took place, but we hardly slowed to dodge the bodies. What I saw had me skidding to a stop.

"Release me!" Astrid yelled.

She was struggling, held in midair by magic. Angry tears streamed down her cheeks. An old hag in an elaborate outfit of layered red and black fabric stood back with a twisted sneer on her face. And Adelaide stood just in front of her, her crimson-hued magic wrapped around the light of my life. Rafe crouched at her feet with his tail tucked between his legs.

Behind them all stood a weeping willow surrounded by a shallow pond. Its leaves glowed brightly, but they were dim in comparison to the ball of pure magic that swirled within the split trunk.

"Adelaide, what are you doing?" I demanded, stepping forward.

Adelaide's pale face went white. Her crimson eyes darted between me, the queen, and the druids emerging from the passage behind us. She and the hag began inching backwards.

"Orion! I—this is not..." she stammered.

The hag's eyes swiveled to me. "Is that him? Is that the fallen star's brat?"

Adelaide lowered her eyes. "Yes, Headwitch."

The hag cackled with glee and rubbed her bony hands together. She looked at me and licked her lips.

Headwitch? *Adelaide's* Headwitch? But what was the Redgrave's leader doing here? I had been under the impression that the covens never worked together!

"Adelaide never defected! She was plotting to kidnap you all this time!" Astrid cried before an invisible gag rendered her mute.

I turned my furious gaze on Adelaide, who refused to meet my eyes. Beside me, the queen growled softly.

"Is this true?" I demanded, my hand straying to the hilt of my sword.

I felt like I had been gutted. Was I such a blind, trusting fool? First Nyra, and now Adelaide? Who was next? Noctus?

"How dare you trespass here!" Queen Rowena snarled. I could feel the powerful magic gathering in her hands. "You will *never* succeed in stealing our magic!"

The Headwitch *tsked*. "As if we have any use for such trifles. But why do you seem so concerned for this cursed halfling?" She cocked her head to one side like an animal, her bloodshot eyes flicking between the queen and Astrid.

She stiffened. The hag grinned.

"I cannot imagine why this one would be important." With a twirl of her hand, her broom sharpened into a spear, which she rested at Astrid's throat. "What do you know of her, Adelaide?"

"She is Queen Rowena's niece," the traitor readily supplied.

"Oh, ho! It seems we have caught an important little mouse." The hag eyed us carefully. "I propose a trade. Hand over the son of the fallen star, and you may keep *this* one. For however long she has left."

"Proposal accepted," the queen answered almost immediately. Despite the murmurs that broke out behind us, she glanced at me from the corner of her eye.

I gave a subtle nod. I would play along with whatever scheme the queen was cooking up—even if there was no scheme at all. Astrid needed to stay *here,* where she could be healed of her curse. I, on the other hand, had no such time constraints.

I stepped forward slowly with my hands raised. My accusatory gaze bored into Adelaide's. Once this was all over, I intended to make her pay dearly for her betrayal.

Adelaide floated Astrid forward. I met her wide eyes, and gave her my best reassuring smile. She shook her head at me, begging me with her eyes not to take another step.

I kept moving, and soon Astrid was behind me. Once I stood in front of the short Headwitch, she reached out to fasten rusted starsteel shackles around my wrists. The instant the cold metal touched my skin, it felt like an insurmountable wall sprang into existence between me and the core of my magic, cutting off my access to it completely. Though I had only just discovered it, I instantly felt the grief of its loss.

I gasped. Was this the so-called corrupted starsteel that had sealed Adelaide's powers?

Adelaide lowered her hands, releasing the magic. The instant she did, and before the hag could lock the shackles, the queen launched spears of ice and wood at the two witches. I yanked my hands away from the corrupted metal at the same moment I heard Astrid cry out in anger.

Rafe jumped in front of Adelaide, shielding her with his body. The projectiles struck him instead, and the force of the blow knocked him straight into the swirling vortex of magic in the heart of the willow. A visceral howl of agony ripped from his chest as the magic enveloped him.

"No! Rafe!" Adelaide cried, lunging forward desperately. I had never seen her show so much emotion, so much fear, before.

"Leave the mutt!" the hag cried, stopping Adelaide from going to him.

She spoke a few garbled words, and a cloud of thick fog exploded from her feet, rapidly filling the whole room. I charged forward desperately, heedless of the danger, and fueled by the desperate fear of losing another loved one at the hands of my betrayer once again.

"Do not let them escape!" the queen commanded. The panic in her voice mirrored my own.

I could hardly even see my own hand in front of my face, but I searched through the area where the three women had just been standing. My hands found only empty air. When the fog finally dissipated a few minutes later, my worst fears were confirmed.

The witches were gone.

And so was Astrid.

Orion

Before I could process what had just happened, someone staggered away from the Sacred Willow with a yell of pain. The unclothed druid male stumbled onto all fours, only to look at his hands in apparent confusion.

Beside me, the queen froze, her gaze riveted to the male, who looked to be around my age, if not a little older. When he looked up, I saw that instead of the blue or green eyes that all druids bore, his eyes were golden.

Just like Rafe's.

And then it clicked. Rafe had been knocked into the Sacred Willow, and this druid had emerged in his place. Had the wolf been a hexed druid this whole time? That would certainly explain the animal's intelligence.

"Cerdan? My son, is that really you?" Queen Rowena stepped forward cautiously, as if she were terrified he would disappear like a mirage.

My lips parted in surprise. "I thought you said you lost your son and husband to the witches long ago?"

"My dear husband had taken our son on patrol with him. The witches attacked, and their bodies were never found," she murmured. "It never occurred to me he had been captured—no ransom was ever demanded of me."

Rafe—or Cerdan—frowned. "My name is Rafe. I have no parents."

The queen looked stricken. "You have no memories of your family?"

"I...I remember very little from before I was a wolf. Just flashes of the forest and gold silk." His golden eyes darted between me and the queen, resting for a heartbeat on her long blonde hair.

She covered her mouth in horror. "They hexed you into a wolf."

Then Rafe growled low in his throat, and as we watched, fur sprouted all over him and his form shifted, until he was a wolf once more. A few druids gasped and clutched at their weapons, but at a wave from their queen, they stood down.

Just as quickly, the fur and fangs retreated until the druid stood before us once more, grinning from ear to ear. Noctus quickly draped a cloak around his shoulders.

"I can control it now," he said with a laugh. "I can speak whenever I want to, and I will not have to wait for Adele to unravel the original hex anymore!" Then he looked around, and his smile faltered. "Where is she?"

"Adelaide and Headwitch Brunhilde of the Redgraves kidnapped Astrid and escaped." I did not attempt to hide the fury in my tone.

His eyes widened. "She left me behind?" When he saw the expression on my face, his golden eyes skittered away from mine.

"Why would you sacrifice yourself to protect that witch?!" Queen Rowena stepped forward.

"Because despite her desire to be accepted, Adele broke the rules to save me. She brought me out of the mountain before that *hag* could use me as a ritual sacrifice. That was why the headwitch kept me alive for so long—she was saving me for a special hex that demanded a special sacrifice."

"And yet, she left you among enemies, those she had betrayed," the queen argued. "Those *you* betrayed."

"Adele must obey her headwitch—she is an outcast within her own coven. From what I overheard, it seems her mother, the previous headwitch, had left the coven defenseless while she sought to capture the fallen star—his mother," Rafe explained, gesturing to me. "In her absence, another coven attacked. Brunhilde took over, and exiled her mother when she failed in her quest. But she also punished the failure's daughter, Adelaide, by sealing her powers with corrupted starsteel. I can understand why she wants to restore her honor and her powers."

"You must have always known why Adelaide came here." It was a statement, not a question.

"Yes."

I rested my hand on the hilt of my sword, trying to wrestle my boiling emotions under control. I knew blaming Rafe was pointless; even if he had had the inclination to tell me the truth, it was not as if he could have spoken to me.

"They will not kill your mate," Rafe said, noting my distress. "They need her alive."

"If Nyra really did make this request of all three covens, then they will have taken Astrid back to Astoria," Noctus agreed. "Adelaide knows you would never abandon her. They will use *her* as bait to catch *you*."

The queen glared at me. "Trouble clings to you like a shadow."

"Trouble that brought you your niece and your son," I spat, then took a deep breath. "Pointing fingers will do no one any good. I will be leaving immediately to rescue her—before the curse takes her from us. Will you be joining me in my efforts or not?"

Queen Rowena glanced at Rafe, before leveling her appraising gaze on me. Before she could answer, however, the sounds of a quickly-approaching party reached our ears. We all drew our weapons on instinct, but I quickly recognized the newcomers.

"Pardon the intrusion, my queen!" Ivy wobbled a quick curtsy before gesturing at the group behind her. "These humans fought off the rest of the witches, who had regrouped and were preparing for a second attack, and requested to speak with our guests."

I grinned as Captain Jolene, Leo, and most of her crew entered the cavernous room, and shot curious glances at the glowing tree. It was good to see some familiar faces.

"Your Majesties," Jolene said with a quick bow, "I am glad to see that you are well." She scanned the room, and her smile flickered. "But where are Astrid, Rafe, and Adelaide?"

I quickly filled them in, and they were understandably shocked and outraged by the news.

"Then my news is of even greater importance," Jolene said grimly, surveying those assembled. "I have received word that the Woman-King has gathered the chief of each Talahari Tribe, for a war council. She means to conquer the entire continent, with the witches as her soldiers and enforcers."

A collective gasp echoed in the cavernous space, and I saw Rafe bare his teeth in an animalistic snarl. The Queen went pale.

"Fortunately, I was able to quickly secure an alliance with Harland's King, thanks in part to the unprecedented increase in attacks from both the tribesmen and the witches. He will stand with us against the Woman-King and her witches," Leo announced proudly.

"I knew you were the right man for the job." Grinning, I clapped him on the back. It felt like a huge weight had been lifted from my chest. I could finally see a glimmer of hope.

"As will my crew and I, plus every starship the Woman-King has crossed," Captain Jolene declared. "Which is most of them."

"If you will have me, I would like to help as well," Rafe chimed in. "I do not want to see Astrid die—and I do not believe Adelaide does, either."

I regarded him cautiously. Would I be a fool to trust him? I noticed he had made no promises when it came to me. But at the moment, I found I did not care. If his presence could distract Adelaide and help me save Astrid, then I would take that chance. "You may come, but know that Noctus will be watching you."

Rafe and Noctus both nodded in acceptance.

I turned to Queen Rowena. "Astrid—your Princess Elowen—told me you had no intention of allying with me. Do you stand by that statement? Or will you help me save your niece and your people, as well as mine?"

The room held its breath, every eye turning to the queen. It felt like the moment of calm before the storm. Our plan, our future, rested on a knife's edge.

"The druids will ally with you and yours, Prince Sterling," Queen Rowena finally declared.

I nodded sagely. "Then let us all save our homes and our loved ones together."

I could only hope we would not be too late.

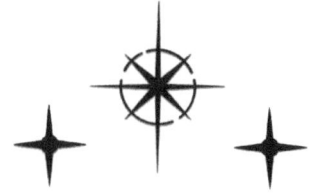

The Adventure Continues...

Orion and Astrid's adventure continues in The Wish King, which is available on Amazon here.

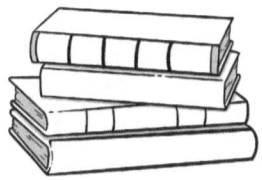

Reviews

If you enjoyed The Druid Queen, I would be forever grateful if you would leave it a review on Amazon here! Reviews make such a huge difference, and I love hearing from my readers!

Want Bonus Chapters?

If you would like to order bookish merch, see character art, and receive updates, free book and audiobook announcements, and release notifications for new book, please sign up here:

Also by K. S. Gerlt

The Werewolf's Mask Series

The Werewolf's Mask

Daughter of Wind and Moonlight

Son of Fang and Fury

Daughter of Steel and Strife

Son of Prejudice and Pride

The Werewolf's Mask Series Coloring Book

The Kingdom of the Stars Series

The Starborn Prince

The Druid Queen

The Wish King

The Witch Queen

About the Author

K. S. Gerlt is an award-winning artist and the author of The Werewolf's Mask series. An avid reader herself, she has always loved diving into the magical worlds within books, from the classics to modern fantasy and adventure. She grew up in Southern California, where her pastimes include horseback riding, ice skating, and painting.

www.ingramcontent.com/pod-product-compliance
Lightning Source LLC
Chambersburg PA
CBHW052045240626
47153CB00006B/2226